"What are we waiting for?" Paige looked at Tanner.

"The eighth round."

A shot hit the water near them.

"Now." When she hesitated, he gave her a push. "Go, go, go."

She sprang from the water and scrambled up the bank, back itching for the bullet she expected. By the time the gunfire resumed, she'd left the river behind and entered the safety of the trees. But she didn't slow down. Tanner was somewhere behind her. She could hear him crashing through the forest.

Finally, he closed the distance between them. "I think we've lost him."

She bent over and sucked in several gulps of air. Tanner seemed as winded as she was.

He looked over at her. "So, who are these guys?"

"I don't know."

He lifted one brow, the gesture filled with doubt. "What are you doing out here? Who are you?"

She searched for an answer. It was there somewhere, but her head hurt too badly to pull it out.

"I...I can't remember."

Carol J. Post writes fun and fast-paced inspirational romantic suspense stories and lives in sunshiny central Florida. She sings and plays the piano for her church and also enjoys sailing, hiking and camping—almost anything outdoors. Her daughters and grandkids live too far away for her liking, so she now pours all that nurturing into taking care of two fat and sassy cats and one highly spoiled dachshund.

Books by Carol J. Post

Love Inspired Suspense

FATAL RECALL

CAROL J. POST

HARLEQUIN® LOVE INSPIRED® SUSPENSE

Recycling programs for this product may not exist in your area.

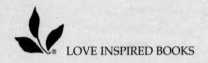

LOVE INSPIRED BOOKS

ISBN-13: 978-1-335-49043-8

Fatal Recall

This edition published by arrangement with Love Inspired Books.

® and TM are trademarks of Love Inspired Books, used under license. Trademarks indicated with ® are registered in the United States Patent and Trademark Office, the Canadian Intellectual Property Office and in other countries.

www.Harlequin.com

Printed in U.S.A.

For I am persuaded, that neither death, nor life, nor angels, nor principalities, nor powers, nor things present, nor things to come, Nor height, nor depth, nor any other creature, shall be able to separate us from the love of God, which is in Christ Jesus our Lord.
–Romans 8:38-39

Acknowledgments

Thank you to all the people who support me
in this career I love:

My wonderful critique partners,
Karen Fleming and Sabrina Jarema,
my eagle-eyed beta reader, Martha "Mom" Post,
my awesome editor, Giselle Regus,
my lovely agent, Nalini Akolekar,
my sister, Kim, for all her help on research,
my sweet, supportive family,
and my loving husband, Chris.

You all are the best!

ONE

The sharp crack of gunfire split the silence.

Tanner Brody froze, his paddle hovering a few inches above the water. A second crack came right after the first.

He released a pent-up breath and shook off the tension. This wasn't one of the scariest areas of Louisville, where he'd grown up. Or even the rough neighborhood there where he'd spent the past eight years as a beat cop. He was on the Nantahala River, at the edge of the Smokies. Someone was hunting—shooting at whatever happened to be in season in North Carolina in early April.

He resumed paddling, adjusting course in time to avoid careening into a rock protruding from the center of the river. Water surged around him, gentle swells tipped in white.

Another shot rang out, and tension spiked through him again. He rolled his shoulders. It would be a while before the *pop* of a rifle didn't send him into action mode.

Eight weeks ago, when his life in Louisville imploded, his friend Colton talked him into moving to Murphy, North Carolina. Six weeks ago, he drained his savings account and made a down payment on a house on two wooded acres. A few days ago, he stuffed everything he owned into a U-Haul and rolled into the drive at almost midnight. He had three weeks to enjoy his freedom. Then he'd start the job he'd landed with Murphy PD.

He wasn't regretting his spur-of-the-moment decision. If there was anyone he trusted, it was Colton. They'd been friends since age thirteen, three of them—him and Kevin and Colton. They'd all shared the same nightmare. Except Colton had gotten out sooner than he and Kevin had.

Tanner reached a calmer section of the river and stopped paddling to take a swig of water. It was still early in the season. Other than a couple sitting at a riverside picnic table some distance back, he hadn't seen another human being.

But rather than feeling lonely, he found the solitude therapeutic. The river flowed around him with a steady *shh* that drowned out all but the calls of the loudest birds and the occasional rumble of a truck moving down the highway a short distance to his right. The firearms had even fallen silent.

He dipped the paddle into the river with smooth, alternating strokes. A roar reached him from somewhere beyond the next bend, warning of an upcoming patch of rapids. Anticipation surged through him. He was ready for whatever the river dished out.

The next moment, a shriek rent the air, short and shrill, as if cut off midstream. He stiffened, the sound like glass across his nerve endings. That was no bird. That was a woman's scream. It came from somewhere to his left, deep in the woods. The internal alarms he'd silenced sounded again. A scream meant trouble, regardless of setting.

He cut a diagonal path toward the river's edge. Once he'd pulled the kayak onto the bank, he checked his supplies. Nothing in the way of first aid. And he'd finished his lunch. He stuffed a granola bar and napkins into his back pockets and grabbed a bottle of water. As he climbed the slope at a stumbling jog, rocks and roots threatened to trip him. Had someone lost their footing and fallen? Or was the scream related to the shots?

He drew in a breath, ready to bellow a loud "Hello," then snapped his mouth closed. Three years in foster care, six in a group home and eight on the force had honed his instincts to a fine point. Right now, something warned him not to give away his position.

For several minutes, he scaled one steep slope, skidded down its opposite side and tackled the next. Briars and other thorny vines grabbed at his clothing and scraped his arms. More than once, his foot found a rock and he caught himself before landing facedown on the hard ground. If he found someone injured, carrying the person over the rugged terrain wouldn't be easy. His best bet would be to call 911.

He stopped and listened for any sign of movement, a moan or whimper. But there was only the whisper of the wind through the trees and the occasional call of a bird. Even the sound of the river had faded and disappeared.

He set out again at the same hurried pace and crested another ridge. Contrast snagged his gaze—faded denim blue against the greens of early spring. He half ran, half slid down the steep grade. As he drew closer, his pulse kicked into overdrive. Trees and underbrush concealed the rest of the body, but what he'd seen were jeans-clad legs ending in well-worn hiking boots.

He dropped to his knees and placed the water bottle on the ground. A woman lay on her right side, eyes closed, lips parted. Her black hair was woven into a thick braid, and her left hand rested near her face. She held remnants of a tan, a band around her ring finger one shade lighter than the rest of her hand. A lightweight jacket was tied around her waist. Judging from the scrapes on her arms, she'd run or rolled through some nasty thorns.

Was she simply unconscious or… No, she didn't have that pallidness of death. He'd seen it on enough occasions to know. The first time was up close and personal at eight years old.

Just to be sure, he placed two fingers against her neck, where her pulse beat strong. He released a breath he hadn't realized he'd been holding. She was alive but needed help. She could have head trauma or internal injuries.

He pulled his phone from his pocket. No service. Not surprising, so far from civilization. His gaze dipped to the woman again, and his jaw tightened. Were the people he'd assumed hunters shooting at her? Had any of the bullets found their mark?

He leaned over her to check her back. There were no patches of moisture on the black tank she wore. She wasn't bleeding from her left side, either.

Maybe the right or front. Twenty minutes had passed since he'd heard her scream. He needed to turn her over. She could have spinal injuries, but if blood was pouring from a bullet wound, she wouldn't last long enough to worry about possible paralysis.

Decision made, he gently rolled her onto her back.

She released a small moan but didn't open her eyes. Her chest rose and fell with a steady rhythm. There were no signs of blood.

He expelled a breath. No one had shot her. Maybe no one had tried. Maybe the shots really had come from hunters.

He looked beyond her to where the ground rose sharply. Had she been hiking and lost her footing, emitting a brief scream of panic as she'd tumbled downward?

It was possible. The Appalachian Trail crossed Highway 19 at the Nantahala Outdoor Center some distance northeast of where they were. He'd seen it when he'd left his truck there, before Colton had taken him to the launch site several miles upstream. Maybe the woman had ventured off the trail.

He gave her a gentle shake. "Can you hear me?"

No response.

Another shake. "Ma'am?"

Her eyes snapped open, the dark brown of their irises almost disappearing into the pupils. She sat up and tried to scramble away. But a boulder at her back stopped her. If someone had been after her, that boulder had likely saved her, shielding her from the view of anyone above.

He held up a hand. "It's okay. I'm not going to hurt you."

Her fear-filled eyes widened further, and she released a blood-chilling scream. The next moment she was on her feet, running away from him. She apparently didn't have any of those spinal injuries he'd worried about.

"Hold up." He took off after her. No way was he leaving her to fend for herself. He'd thought she might be a hiker who'd wandered off the trail and fallen. Now his gut told him it was a lot more. And he always listened to his gut.

He closed the distance between them. It wasn't difficult. Her balance was off, her gait faltering. He wrapped both arms around her from behind, clamping a hand over her mouth to cut off a second scream. Though she was a good head shorter than him, she was firm and athletic. He could tell she was an outdoor kind of woman, based on the build and the tan.

An elbow came back to jab him in the ribs at the same time a boot caught him in the shin. He released a grunt, thankful she wasn't functioning at 100 percent. When he tightened his hold, she struggled harder. The other elbow shot back, but this time he avoided it.

"Stop fighting me." He hissed the words in her ear. "I won't hurt you. I came to help you. I'm…" He hesitated. "A nice guy."

He'd almost said *cop*. But if it was her own bad deeds that had gotten her into trouble, gaining her trust as law enforcement wasn't going to happen.

"We need to get you out of here. But no more screaming. We don't want to give whoever you're running from any more hints of your whereabouts." He paused, letting his words penetrate her panic. "I'm taking my hand away now."

He loosened his hold but didn't relax his vigilance. If she tried to scream or run, he'd have her back in his embrace before she could draw another breath.

She turned to face him. Her eyes still held wildness, and she looked ready to bolt. But she nodded agreement.

"I'm going to get you to safety."

He retrieved the water, and when he offered it to her, she drank almost all of it without stopping to breathe.

While she finished, he looked around them. He needed to get her medical aid as soon as possible. Since he'd found her unconscious, she obviously had a head injury. Without cell service, he had no option but to walk her out of the woods. Once they made it to the highway, they could flag someone down and catch a ride to the Nantahala Outdoor Center. After an ambulance arrived, he'd ask a Good Samaritan to give him a ride back to where he'd left Colton's kayak.

Of course, that was all contingent on someone stopping. Actually, there was a more serious problem. If someone was after the woman, he'd expect her to hike toward the highway. They could walk into a trap. Maybe the kayak was their best option.

After he took her empty bottle, he waited while she untied her jacket and slipped her arms into the sleeves. Then he extended his arm, palm up. "Let me help you."

Her gaze dipped to his hand, and indecision filled her eyes. She'd apparently experienced something traumatic. Otherwise she wouldn't have been so terrified of him.

As they walked, she kept her hand in his. Her grip was firm. Strength had to be a good sign. Or maybe the firm grip meant she felt unsteady. Whatever the case, she wasn't much of a conversationalist.

He offered her a friendly smile. "I'm Tanner." His tone was just above a whisper.

One side of her mouth lifted a sliver. "Hi, Tanner."

She didn't give him her name. Maybe his hunch she might be running from crimes of her own was dead-on.

Right now, that didn't matter. His responsibility was to get her to safety, which meant a hospital so she could be checked out. It would be up to local authorities to decide what to do with her after release.

As they walked, he kept scanning the woods. He'd left his pistol in the glove box of his Silverado, never dreaming he'd need it kayaking. What he wouldn't give to have a weapon now. The three-inch blade on his multi-tool didn't count.

When they reached the river, he heaved a sigh of relief. They'd made it. Almost. He still had to get her to a working phone. Fortunately, whoever was after her likely wouldn't look for her on the river.

After lowering the kayak into the water, he helped her into the front and took the seat at the rear. Colton had bought the small boat with his wife in mind, so it was a two-seater.

"Keep an eye out." The command was probably unnecessary. He couldn't see the woman's face, but her head slowly pivoted side to side.

A half minute later, they rounded the bend, and a long stretch of white water lay ahead. Theirs was the only boat in either direction. In another month or two, activity would pick up, but April was early. Though the sun was shining, the air still held some bite.

Over the next several minutes, he split his attention between navigating the rapids and scanning the trees that bordered both sides of the river. A gasp drew his attention to the front. The woman had twisted and sat looking over her right shoulder.

He followed her gaze. "Did you see something?"

"I thought I did. Now I don't."

He didn't, either. Without slowing his pace, he gave hard looks in that direction. Pines, firs and other evergreens stood interspersed among trees budding with new spring growth.

Then there was movement. Something dark, out of place with the greens of nature. He continued his powerful strokes, casting repeated glances over his right shoulder.

Something shifted, and the dark area became a black shirt or jacket. There was more movement. Then a flash. A glint.

Like the sun reflecting off something metallic.

Someone had a gun. It was likely aimed at them.

And he had about one second to react.

Three cracks split the air in rapid succession. A second later, she hit the water face-first, driving it into her mouth and up her nose. Its icy chill engulfed her, and the current dragged her downstream, slamming her body into submerged rocks. When she surfaced, she gasped for air between fits of coughing. Tanner was nearby, being carried downstream at the same speed as her, one arm looped over the side of the kayak.

"Get to the edge." He gained his footing, then turned to roll the kayak onto its side.

"What are you trying to do, drown me?" Even as the words spilled out, she knew better. Gunfire had reverberated around them as he'd tackled her and pulled her overboard.

He ignored her outburst. "Keep down and stay out of sight."

The worst of the rapids was behind them; the current at the river's edge was more manageable. More shots rang out, none of them finding their mark. Which was good. A bullet would sail through plastic as easily as a hot knife through butter.

As they approached the bank, everything fell eerily silent. Moments later, gunfire again rent the air. A hole appeared near the back of the boat. Of the next four shots, two hit their target. One narrowly missed Tanner.

He tilted his head toward the bank. "We're going to use that for protection."

She cast a glance over her shoulder. An old hardwood had lost its grip at the edge of the river and toppled over, its roots a vertical tangled mass six feet in diameter.

The assailant fired two more shots. Tanner stared at her, eyes intense. "When I give the word, scramble up the bank, staying as close to the downed tree as you can. Then run into the woods without looking back."

When the water wasn't much more than a foot deep, she dropped from a crouch to her hands and knees. The bank was within arm's reach.

She looked at Tanner. "What are we waiting for?"

"The eighth round."

"Huh?"

Before he could respond, a shot hit the water near them.

"Now."

When she hesitated, he gave her a push. "Go, go, go."

She sprang from the water and scrambled up the bank, back itching for the bullet she expected. By the time the gunfire resumed, she'd left the river behind and entered the safety of the trees on its opposite slope.

But she didn't slow down. Tanner was somewhere behind her. She could hear him crashing through the forest.

Finally, he closed the distance between them. "I think we've lost him."

She bent over and sucked in several gulps of air. Tanner looked to be in great shape, definitely a man who frequented the gym. But he was as winded as she was.

He leaned against a tree and pulled his phone from his pocket. "No service. But thanks to the waterproof case, it looks like it survived our impromptu swim." He slid it back into his pocket. "So, who are these guys?"

"I don't know."

He lifted one brow, the gesture filled with doubt. "What are you doing out here?"

She searched for an answer. It was there somewhere, but her head hurt too badly to pull it out. "I can't remember."

Tanner frowned. "You forget where you put your car keys, not why you're alone in the woods with men shooting at you."

"I said I don't know. Okay? Just leave me alone." She stalked off in a different direction. Her head was killing her and focusing was pretty much impossible. She didn't need some stranger giving her a hard time.

He fell into step beside her. "I'm trying to help you. Do you have a name?"

She studied his face, as if the answer would somehow be there. What she found were piercing green eyes under a head of soft brown hair and a square jaw covered by a day's worth of stubble. Not a single hint as to her identity.

She shook her head. "I'm sure I do. I just can't remember what it is right now."

He stopped to stare at her. "You're serious." Whatever doubt she'd seen had turned to concern. "What about ID?"

She patted her pockets. Nothing in her jeans pockets, front or back. One jacket pocket was empty. The other… She pulled out a small wooden box, rectangular in shape. It looked handmade, with perfectly cut pieces of wood joined together, a polished patchwork of varying shades.

She turned it over. A minuscule crack circled the longer sides, close to the end. A seam between pieces of wood? Or the edges of a drawer? She tugged at it, then frowned. If it was a drawer, it wasn't budging.

Tanner held out a hand. "Let me try. It's probably swollen from getting wet."

She handed him the box, then stood next to him while he pried and pulled. Finally, he'd worked it open enough to look inside. It was empty, except for some bits of dried leaves. Tobacco?

Tanner brought it to his nose, and his brows knit. When she gave it her own test, a knot formed in her stomach. It wasn't tobacco. It was pot.

She shook her head. "This isn't mine."

Tanner cocked a brow. He didn't believe her.

Of course not. How could she know she didn't smoke pot when every memory had been wiped clean? She didn't have an answer for *how* she knew, just that she did. "I don't know why I have this, but I can guarantee you if this box held joints, they weren't mine." She frowned. "I have some pretty strong emotions right now, and they're not good."

She took what he held and closed the drawer. "Whoever the box belonged to, I'm keeping it." She slid her hand over the varnished surface, then slipped the item back into her pocket. "This is all I've got. Nothing that offers any hint about who I am."

A chill ripped through her, and a shudder shook her shoulders. He stepped closer to run his hands briskly up and down her arms. "I hope it's just the wet clothes and you're not going into shock. We need to get you to a doctor, pronto."

He took her hand and resumed walking, his gait stiff but fast. "We'll veer to the left, then double back. We should be able to avoid whoever is after you but still reach the highway."

She nodded. She had no idea where they were. Ever since her panic subsided enough to think straight, she'd tried to recall the last thing that had happened. An hour later, she still couldn't remember. And her head felt as if someone had clamped it into a vise.

Whether or not she was in shock, she was freezing. Her drenched jeans leached warmth from her body with every step, and her wet jacket flopped against her torso, pounding the chill deeper.

It wasn't going to get better. The sun was resting too low to dry clothes or warm bodies. They probably had less than an hour of daylight left. If they didn't make it out soon, they'd be spending the night in the woods. Another shiver passed through her.

He squeezed her hand, and she gave him a shaky smile. "Thank you for everything. I hate to think what would've happened if you hadn't come along."

"I'm glad I was there."

She cast him another glance. "What did you mean by 'the eighth round'?"

"I was counting the shots. There was a gap after the first eight, then another gap after the next eight.

Whoever is after you is using a pistol with a magazine that holds eight cartridges. After the eighth shot, he'd have to refill cartridges or at least change magazines."

Another shot sounded, and bark exploded from a tree not six feet away. She bit off the scream that leaped up her throat.

Tanner broke into a run, pulling her with him. If their original path took them farther from civilization, so did this one, because they were headed in roughly the same direction. Her hopes of making it out before dark died a quick and sure death.

They crested a ridge and made a diagonal path down the other side. Without slowing, they climbed another slope, then descended, adjusting direction again. The sun sank lower and the shadows lengthened.

Tanner stopped and pulled her down behind a fallen tree. "I think we lost him again."

She sucked in several gulps of air. "I hope you're right."

Their pursuer had firepower, but she and Tanner had agility and stamina. At least Tanner did. Whatever stamina she had was fading fast.

She looked over his shoulder, where the sun had dipped behind the trees sometime ago. Overhead, the sky had darkened to gray blue. Soon it would turn to navy, then black.

He followed her gaze. "We shouldn't wander around in the dark. There are thousands of acres of forest out here."

Her chest tightened. Spending the night alone in the woods with a strange man couldn't be smart, no matter how nice he seemed. Besides, now that the sun was going down, the temperature was dropping, and she was already cold. But Tanner was right.

He pulled a flattened granola bar from his pocket. "Dinner. I'll share it with you." He removed it from the wrapper, and when he'd split it, he gave her the larger piece.

Her stomach rumbled. "I'm sure it'll be the best granola bar I've ever eaten." She hesitated. Did she actually remember eating a granola bar? Could she recall *any* sensory experiences? No, she couldn't. She heaved a sigh. How would she ever function as an independent adult if she couldn't call up something as simple as having a snack?

She shook off the concerns. Only a few hours had passed since she'd hit her head. She needed to give it time. She broke off a small piece of the bar and put it in her mouth, savoring it before swallowing. If she spread it out, maybe it would fill her up.

A few seconds later, Tanner brushed his empty hands together. His portion was gone in two bites. She shouldn't have accepted the larger half.

"Have some of this."

"I'm fine." He patted his stomach. "That totally hit the spot."

"You're lying." She split what she had left and held out her hand. "Take it."

"You need to keep up your strength." He pushed himself to his feet. "Rest while I try to find a semiprotected place to spend the night."

After watching him walk away, she took another bite. Even breaking it into small pieces, the bar went too fast and came nowhere near filling the empty hole in her stomach. She'd eaten almost twice what Tanner had. *He must be starving.*

Gratitude welled up inside her, thankfulness toward Tanner and whatever force had sent him to her. The chance of anyone finding her before her attempted killer was slim to none. The odds of someone like Tanner finding her were closer to the "none" side. She was really lucky.

Not lucky, blessed.

Where had that thought come from? She apparently had some kind of religious background. She searched her mind, trying to pull out some snatch of memory.

Nothing. If the index cards were there, they were all blank.

She rubbed her arms through the damp fabric of the jacket. The temperature seemed to be dropping by the minute. What she wouldn't give for a set of dry clothes.

Leaving her arms crossed in front of her, she rested her head against an upward-jutting branch and closed her eyes. Now that the immediate danger was over, fatigue was setting in. She could use a nap almost as much as a change of clothes.

The rhythmic crunch of footsteps in dried leaves brought her fully alert. Tanner was twenty feet in front of her, closing the distance. Relief flitted across his features. "You looked like you'd fallen asleep."

She matched his soft tone. "Almost. I only needed another couple of minutes. Along with a warm blanket."

"I wish I could help with the blanket. But you probably shouldn't sleep. I'm no doctor, but I know when someone has a head injury, you're supposed to keep them awake."

She frowned. "For how long?"

"Since I don't know, we'll go with 'as long as possible.'"

"Great."

"The good news is, I think I know how to keep us somewhat warm for the night."

He held out a hand, and she let him pull her to her feet. After leading her a short distance away, he pointed. The ground sloped upward on each side, with a trough between. A good-size tree had fallen and lay across it at a sharp angle.

"We can burrow in under that dead hemlock. There's already a thick bed of leaves. Since it hasn't rained, it's nice and dry. I'll gather branches to block us in the rest of the way and keep out any unwanted guests."

She almost asked him what he meant by "unwanted guests," then decided she'd rather not know.

"We've also got water. Listen."

She lifted her chin. Behind the rustle of leaves and buzz of insects, a trickle reached her from somewhere in the distance.

When they arrived at the little creek, she dropped to her knees. The water was cold and tasted so good. Too many hours had passed since she'd finished the bottle Tanner had given her.

After drinking their fill, they headed back. She helped him gather limbs, then watched as he positioned them, leaving a single opening protected by one of the hemlock's branches. He completed the last of the work by moonlight. When he finished, her teeth were chattering.

"Let's get you out of this night air."

She dropped to her hands and knees, then crawled downhill to the trough. It was narrow, just wide enough for a single body. But it was plenty long enough to allow a respectable distance between them.

After choosing the space to the left, she stretched out on her back and nestled into the leaves. Moonlight shone through the branches overhead in tiny geometric shapes. It wasn't any warmer inside than outside, but getting out of the nighttime breeze helped. Even the hard ground wasn't that uncomfortable. Knowing Tanner, he'd probably added some extra cushion. But it was still going to be a long damp night. She crossed her arms over her torso, trying to ward off the chill.

As Tanner maneuvered his body into the shelter, alarms went off. She struggled to silence them. If any man deserved trust, Tanner did. But trust didn't come easily in her current state. Maybe it didn't come easily in her normal state, either.

"Are you warm enough?" His voice sounded close.

"Better."

Still in a crawling position, he gathered some smaller hemlock branches he'd cut previously and reached over her head to lay them across her torso.

"Thanks."

"You're welcome. If there's anything else I can do, let me know."

"Other than the blanket."

"Other than the blanket." His tone held a smile. Leaves crinkled and dried twigs cracked as he positioned himself a few feet away. There was nothing solid between them, but he was giving her space. A true gentleman.

She smiled into the darkness. "You did good today. What are you anyway? Ex-military? Survivalist? Former Boy Scout?"

He laughed. "None of the above. Why?"

"The way you've handled everything. Evading the bad guy. Getting us to safety. Putting this together. I'm impressed." She shook her head. "I mean, who thinks to count rounds when they're being shot at?"

He gave another soft chuckle. "I'm a cop, and I have a lot of outdoor hobbies."

She lifted her brows, her interest piqued. "What kind of hobbies?"

"Camping, hiking, canoeing, kayaking. And some other activities that aren't so tame."

"Like what?"

"Rock climbing, sandboarding, parasailing, whitewater rafting. Class five, of course. There's a group of four of us—three of us that do adventures together once or twice a year."

"Three of you now?" She grinned. "Did you lose one?"

"We've got a backpacking trip planned for Colorado this summer, probably just Bryce and me. Colton's occupied these days with a wife and kid."

She frowned. He'd continued without acknowledging her question. Maybe something terrible really had happened to the fourth guy.

He proceeded to relay some of his experiences. Finally, he stopped. "I'm sorry, I'm monopolizing the conversation."

"That's okay. What consists of my life story right now, you've witnessed. So talk on."

She enjoyed listening to him. His tales were interesting, his voice soothing, with a liquid smoothness and rich timbre. As he talked, her thoughts grew more random, and she drifted on the fringes of oblivion.

Tanner paused. "Hey, you're not falling asleep, are you?"

"Mmm-hmm." She didn't open her eyes.

"Seriously. Wake up."

She forced her eyes open. "Are you going to keep me awake all night?"

"I'm going to try."

That probably wasn't a bad idea. She needed to stay alert. For all she knew Tanner could be an ax murderer.

That's not what she felt, though. The vibes she got from him were all positive.

But who was she to make that determination?

How could she trust her gut when she couldn't even remember who she was?

TWO

The air was cold and damp. No matter what she did, she couldn't get warm.

She drew her legs up, curling into a fetal position. It didn't help. The damp chill had permeated every cell. When she reached for her comforter, her fingers wrapped around a stick.

She came awake with a gasp. A hand clamped down hard on her mouth, pinching off her nose at the same time. Her heart stopped, then kick-started in triple time.

Her eyes adjusted to the semidarkness of the room. Someone leaned over her, his head silhouetted against the speckled backdrop of the ceiling.

Tanner. His lips were compressed as if to shush her, but no sound came out.

Footfalls sounded a short distance away. The events of the prior day slammed into her with the force of a tidal wave. If not for the hand clamped over her mouth, she'd have sucked in another gasp.

Tanner apparently recognized awareness in her eyes, because he slowly removed his hand.

The footsteps crunched closer, the tread heavy. "I know you're here somewhere. I heard you."

A heavy silence fell. The guy had stopped, probably studying his surroundings. Had she and Tanner left evidence of their presence? Broken limbs? Trampled underbrush?

God, please don't let him find us.

The spontaneous prayer brought her up short. Did she have that kind of relationship with God, where she could send up a silent plea and expect to get an answer?

Maybe not. A panicked prayer in a moment of duress didn't mean anything.

The man started moving again. "You might as well give up. I'm gonna find you." He walked away and circled back, approaching on the other side. Then the footsteps retreated.

She lay stock-still for what seemed like forever, scarcely daring to breathe. Finally, Tanner crept from their bunker. When she crawled out behind him, he was looking around, eyes alert. A shiver shook her shoulders. What she could see of the sky to her right looked a little lighter than the rest, but it would be some time before the sun traveled high enough to warm the air.

Tanner looked down at her. "He's gone."

She expeled a breath. *Thank You.* Wherever the answer had come from, someone deserved the recognition.

"It sounded like he headed toward the river." Tanner was still whispering. "I'm hoping he's given up looking for us. When we get back to civilization, we'll figure out our next step."

She nodded. He'd said "we." Maybe he didn't plan to dump her at the nearest hospital or police department.

"Are you thirsty?"

"And hungry." She gave him a weak smile. "I don't

suppose you have another squished granola bar hiding anywhere."

"'Fraid not."

As she followed him toward the creek, she cast repeated glances over her shoulder. As long as the shooter didn't double back, they should be all right.

"I'd promise you a steak dinner tonight but I'm afraid the fare is going to be hospital cuisine. They're going to want to run tests, probably keep you overnight."

Though she didn't look forward to a hospital stay, having her memory wiped out was disconcerting enough to go along with whatever Tanner suggested.

He stepped to the side to walk next to her. "Have you remembered anything since yesterday?"

"Nothing. But I woke up this morning." Tanner's concerns about her falling into a concussion-induced coma were for naught. Until that final stretch before dawn, her sleep had been too fitful. Besides being cold, she couldn't find a good position. The ground had seemed harder with every passing hour.

He picked up a stick and broke a piece off its end. "You need a name."

"Any ideas?"

He walked in silence, his expression thoughtful. "You don't look like a Sarah or a Millie or a Priscilla."

"Why not?"

"Those names are too…" His voice trailed off as he struggled to come up with the right adjective.

"Soft and feminine?"

He winced.

"It's okay. I'm wearing jeans, hiking boots and a messy braid. I don't look like a Priscilla."

"So no soft names." He broke off another piece of

the stick he held and tossed it. "You need something strong—something implying athleticism, competence, self-sufficiency."

She quirked a brow, not sure how he came up with the last two descriptors. She'd have been in a pickle without him. But since she'd eluded her assailant until knocking herself unconscious, she had to have some level of competence.

They reached the creek, and she knelt next to it. "How about Katrina?"

He loomed over her, wiggling his brows. It didn't matter what he called her. Anything they came up with would be temporary until someone identified her or she regained her memory.

"You don't look like a Katrina." He dropped down next to her. "Or maybe you do. Kat for short."

"Alrighty, then. I guess I'm Kat." She didn't feel any connection to the name. Of course, she didn't expect to.

After sipping several scoops of water, they straightened. Her stomach growled, and she pressed a hand to her waistline. Judging from the condition of the trees, it was early spring. Not the time of year to find edible berries.

She stood and let her gaze follow the meandering creek. A short way down on the opposite bank, spots of yellow stood out against patches of green.

She moved that direction, picking up speed as she got closer. She'd been right. A patch of dandelions grew alongside the water.

"Kat?" Tanner's footsteps sounded behind her.

She stepped onto a rock in the middle of the creek. A second step put her on the opposite bank. "Breakfast."

"What?"

She indicated the plants with a wave of her arm.

"It's not bacon and scrambled eggs, but it should help to curb the hunger."

After plucking several blooms and a handful of leaves, she tried one of each. The slight crunch and sweetness of the flower blended with the earthy, bitter taste of the greens.

Tanner watched her with his eyebrows drawn together, his lips in a straight line. "Are you sure that's safe?"

"Positive. Ever heard of dandelion tea?"

"Yeah, but parts of some plants are poisonous."

"Not dandelion." She wasn't sure how she knew that, but she did. "Come and get some."

Tanner continued to watch her, doubt radiating from him. She understood. She couldn't expect him to trust his life to her ability to identify edible wild plants when she couldn't remember her own name. She couldn't explain it herself. Some knowledge was still accessible, but her experiences were exiled to a remote island in her brain, the bridge to access it blown to smithereens.

Finally, Tanner crossed the creek to pick some dandelions for himself. He chewed and swallowed his first bite. "Hmm, like salad for breakfast."

When they'd had their fill, Tanner knelt for another drink, then straightened. "I think the bad guy's way ahead of us, but we'll keep our eyes and ears open."

She stuffed her hands into her jacket pockets, still slightly damp from yesterday's swim. Her right hand found the box, and she pulled it out. It didn't stir her memory any better than it had before.

"Other than the clothes I'm wearing, this is the only thing connecting me to my past, as shaky as that connection is." The box probably didn't even belong to her.

Tanner nodded. "It's good you're keeping it. It might help trigger your memory."

"I agree." She slid the box back into her pocket and looked beyond Tanner, where the sun worked its way upward in a hazy sky.

"We're north of Highway 19. If we head south, we should reach it eventually."

She set out walking beside him. "What about your kayak?"

"It's actually my friend's. The shooter might be waiting for us, so I'll get it later with a police escort."

"That's a good—" Her sentence ended in a squeak as her ankle twisted with a sharp crack. Pain shot halfway up her leg.

Tanner's quick reflexes kept her from falling. "Are you okay?"

She tested her weight. It was painful, but nothing she couldn't handle.

Tanner led her to a downed tree. "Sit here while I look for a walking stick."

"That'll delay us. I'll be fine."

"Since the guy with the gun is somewhere ahead of us, this'll put more distance between us and him."

She lowered herself to the rough bark and watched Tanner circle the area, picking up and discarding sticks. Finally, he found one that suited his purposes.

He pulled something from his pocket, too thick to be a pocketknife. Instead, the metal case held an array of gadgets. He selected a blade and spent several minutes slicing off small limbs and whittling a smooth grip area. Finally, he stood and tested it.

"Here you go."

She pulled herself to her feet. "This is awesome. Thank you."

"It was a piece of cake with my handy little multi-tool." He raised the mentioned item, blade still extended.

As she stared at the object, a memory stirred. A man flew backward, cracking his head on the concrete sidewalk. His assailant leaped on top of him, one hand splayed on his chest, the other holding a switchblade at his throat. Blood beaded along the razor-sharp edge, and the man's eyes held the terror of someone looking death in the face.

"Kat? Are you okay?" Tanner's voice sounded far away.

She squeezed her eyes shut, willing the image to disappear.

"Tell me what you see."

She swallowed the bile pushing its way up her throat. "A knife. Someone being attacked."

"Do you know who?"

She tried to focus. The man was thin and wiry, clad in a tank-style undershirt, tattoos marking his arms, neck and chest. If he was someone she knew, memories of him were buried with the rest of her past.

"All I saw was a brief flash—the man, the knife." And the hand holding it.

"Is it possible you witnessed a murder and that's why someone is after you?"

She gave a jerky nod. "Maybe."

What Tanner said was possible. Even logical.

But that wasn't what happened. She was sure of it.

Because the hand holding the knife had been her own.

Tanner put the multi-tool away and slipped a palm under her left elbow. Her face had lost three shades of color.

"Are you sure you're okay?"

The quick bob of her head wasn't convincing. The fact that she was already recovering her memory was good. The shock it gave her wasn't.

She set out walking, favoring her right ankle, and he fell into step beside her.

"If you need to stop, let me know."

"Thanks, but the stick helps. I'm anxious to get out of these woods." Her eyes held hesitation. "Where will you be taking me?"

"Bryson City. The police department, then the hospital." He'd studied a map of the area, and it was the nearest town. In fact, the Nantahala Outdoor Center had a Bryson City address.

Her jaw tightened, and her brows drew together. Did she have a fear of hospitals? Or was it going to the police that worried her?

"We need to file a report." The moment someone shot at them, he'd scratched his plans for putting her in an ambulance and letting the EMTs haul her away. "There's a chance the police can help us figure out who you are, especially if your prints are in the system."

"You think I might be a criminal?" She smiled, but there was tension behind it.

He shrugged. "Lots of people get fingerprinted for their jobs. It doesn't mean they're criminals."

She stared straight ahead, apparently not convinced. He understood her reservations. It was a scary proposition. She could learn she's a fugitive and be led away in handcuffs. With all she'd been through, he hoped that wasn't the case.

She heaved a sigh. "However it turns out, it'll be a relief to find out who I am."

"Someone's probably reported you missing by now."

"Maybe." She held out her left hand, palm down. "Looks like I wore a ring long enough to tan around it. I don't know if it was a wedding or an engagement ring. Or why I no longer have it on."

As they walked, the sun climbed higher, burning off the haze and warming the air. Finally, she shrugged out of the jacket. As she tied it around her waist, muscles worked beneath a pale gray design, a tattoo that looked about two laser treatments away from removal.

He touched her upper arm. "Does this trigger any memories?"

She turned her head to see what he'd indicated. "Not at all."

He'd noticed the tattoo yesterday, before she'd put her jacket on. It was a fairly elaborate crown, a common gang symbol. That connection would help the police identify her. Chances were good she had a record.

Whatever affiliations she'd had, she'd likely gotten out, a feat in itself. Otherwise she wouldn't have borne the pain and expense of trying to have the symbol removed.

"How about this?" He traced a three-inch scar on her forearm.

"It looks like an old cut, but I don't remember where I got it."

"It'll come to you eventually. You've already regained one memory."

She sat and unlaced her right boot. As she removed it, she winced. When she peeled off her sock, he frowned. A discolored area wrapped the bottom of her ankle and spread across her foot toward her toes. Tissue had tried to swell against the tightly laced boot, leaving reddened grooves.

"Too bad we don't have some ice for that."

"It'll be all right. I'm sure I've experienced worse." She indicated her upper arm with her other hand. "This, for example."

"I agree." As he and Kevin had aged out of the system, they'd talked about having an eagle tattooed over their right pecs, signifying freedom. Kevin had followed through. Tanner hadn't. He really didn't like needles. From everything he'd heard, he wouldn't like lasers any better.

Kat was one tough lady. She'd sustained a head injury, slept on the ground in damp clothes, gone hungry and walked the past three hours on a sprained ankle. All without complaint. She was more resilient than a lot of men he knew.

After a brief rest, she put her sock and shoe back on, then stood. But instead of resuming the hike, she uprooted some nearby plants. Onion-like greens grew from small, light-colored bulbs. She brought them to her nose. "Wild garlic."

When she handed him one, he sniffed it. Though not as strong as expected, it still held that distinctive scent.

She munched on the green stems, then peeled the outer layer to expose the clean bulb. After removing the roots with her thumbnail, she popped the bulb into her mouth.

He did the same. The dandelions were long digested, and he was starved. He'd never been a dainty eater. Even before his postadolescent growth spurt, when he'd weighed one hundred pounds soaking wet, it hadn't been for lack of nutrition. His small size had made him a target for bullies in the foster and group homes, so he'd always eaten like a horse. It eventually paid off.

Kat picked up her walking stick and resumed their trek. Soon, the sound of moving water reached them. Rather than the trickle of a creek, it was a constant barrage of sound, a steady *shh* that grew louder as they walked.

"Hear that?"

"I do." She gave him a cautious smile. "I'm just not looking forward to wading across. I don't feel like getting wet again *or* fighting that current."

"We may not have to. If we come out a mile or so upstream from where we left the kayak, we'll miss it. Where I launched, the river flows on the other side of the road, then crosses under a bridge."

A truck engine rumbled in the distance, increasing in volume, then fading. When they headed down the last slope, the river lay in front them. To the right, it curved to disappear under a bridge.

They covered the final yards, then stopped at the shoulder to look both directions. Traffic was nonexistent. To the left, Highway 19 stretched toward Bryson City. The Nantahala Outdoor Center was about five miles away. If someone would give them a ride, they'd save an hour and a half of walking. For Kat's sake, he hoped some Good Samaritans were traveling on 19.

As they crossed the two-lane highway, a white pickup truck moved toward them. Kat held out a thumb, and the truck barreled past. Five other vehicles did the same. He didn't blame the drivers. Picking up hitchhikers was a good way to get oneself killed.

When a low rumble sounded behind them, he turned to watch a box truck approach. He held up a hand to flag down the driver. The truck slowed and the right-turn signal came on. Tanner's pulse kicked up.

The vehicle eased to a stop, an auto parts delivery truck. Tanner opened the passenger door and helped Kat in, then slid in behind her.

"Where you headed?" Reflective sunglasses hid the driver's eyes.

"Nantahala Outdoor Center. It's not far, but five miles on a sprained ankle can feel like forty." He tilted his head toward Kat.

"Not fun." His straight salt-and-pepper hair was pulled into a ponytail beneath a New York Jets ball cap, and he exuded a relaxed friendliness.

Tanner checked his phone again. Still no service. He'd rather have the police there, or at least en route, when he and Kat arrived. Since they'd been in a kayak, the Nantahala Outdoor Center was the most logical place to end up. The shooter could be waiting for them.

But he wouldn't expect them to arrive in an auto parts delivery truck. By the time he figured it out, Tanner would have his pistol in hand.

The driver slowed for a curve. "How'd you guys get so far from your truck anyway? There aren't any hiking trails out this way."

Tanner looked past Kat to study the man, debating how much to tell him. It didn't take him long. If the driver was a threat, they'd already know it. He was sticking his neck out for them. He needed to know the situation.

"We were kayaking, then wound up running from a guy with a gun."

His mouth went slack. "Have you called the police?"

"We will as soon as we get service."

As they approached the Outdoor Center, the driver reached into a pocket on his door and laid a pistol in his lap. "Just in case."

Tanner scanned the roadside. No one seemed to be lurking. Two cars sat in the parking lot, both empty, the occupants likely inside the building. His Silverado waited at the far end. He pointed it out, and the driver stopped in the next space.

"I'll make sure you get away okay."

"Thanks, man." Tanner slipped a soggy bill into the guy's hand, then climbed from the truck.

Kat cast a glance over her shoulder as she slid across the seat. "God bless you."

The driver smiled. "He already has."

Tanner raised his brows at the semireligious conversation between two unlikely candidates—Kat, with the remains of her gang tattoo, and the truck driver, with his shades and ponytail.

Two of the foster homes he'd landed in had been religious, with a list of dos and don'ts that would stretch from Louisville to Nashville. He couldn't quote it from memory, but he was pretty sure ponytails and tattoos were on the "don't" side.

While the delivery guy waited, Tanner let Kat into the passenger seat of the Silverado and removed his Glock from the glove box. Now the playing field was a little more level.

As he circled around to the driver's side, he continued to scan the area. Even when he pulled onto Highway 19, with the delivery truck behind him, he still didn't relax. He probably wouldn't until he and Kat were seated inside the police station at some officer's desk.

He glanced in his rearview mirror. The truck was

still behind him, keeping up in spite of the seemingly endless series of S curves. Finally, the highway straightened out and widened to four lanes. Tanner chose the right one. The truck driver did, too. A red van behind them moved into the left. Within moments, it overtook him and sped past.

Another vehicle traveled in that lane, also, too far back to identify the make. Instead of accelerating, the driver matched the speed of those in the slower lane, forcing others to go around him.

Tension crept across Tanner's shoulders. Was someone intentionally keeping them in sight while remaining far enough away to avoid identification?

"So, we're headed to Bryson City." Kat's words broke into his thoughts. "To the police department."

"Yeah." The other direction would have taken them to Andrews, then Murphy. Murphy had a hospital. He'd seen it—Murphy Medical Center. He didn't want to risk leading anyone to his new hometown. But unless Kat made an amazing recovery over the next twenty-four hours, she'd need someone to keep an eye on her.

She wasn't his responsibility. But until she figured out where she belonged, she wasn't anybody's responsibility. He couldn't just dump her. The role of protector was too deeply ingrained.

He shifted position to pull his phone from his pocket, then handed it to Kat. "See if we have service yet."

"Two bars."

"Can you pull up directions to the Bryson City Police Department?"

Her thumbs flew over the screen. A half minute later, a computerized voice informed him that he was on the fastest route.

When he looked at her again, she was chewing her lower lip.

"You okay?"

She sighed. "What if I've done something terrible and they arrest me?"

"You look more like a victim than a criminal."

She gave him a weak smile. "Thanks."

As they approached town, he took a brush from the console and ran it through his hair. When he started to put it back, she stopped him.

"Do you mind?"

"Go right ahead."

She removed the elastic band from the end of the braid and slipped it around her wrist. "If I'm going to jail, I at least want to look halfway decent."

After working the tresses loose, she shook them out, then went to work with the brush. Soon her hair flowed over both shoulders in shiny black waves, falling all the way to her waist. Even after spending the last two days in the woods, she was beautiful.

Not that it mattered to him. Those were the ones to worry about. The beautiful ones. Especially around deceitful best friends.

Up ahead, Highway 74 broke from 19, veering off to the right. As Tanner took the exit, remaining on 74, he checked his mirrors. The auto parts truck followed him. So did the car he'd been watching. That didn't mean anything. Highway 74 was well traveled.

At the instruction of the GPS, he moved into the left lane. The truck driver flew past with a wave and two toots of his horn. The car followed him and Kat. He forced himself to relax. Maybe the driver had business in Bryson City, too.

"Is everything okay?"

He glanced in the rearview mirror again. "We might have a tail." At her gasp, he continued, "Don't turn around. Just be ready to call 911."

"According to the GPS, we're less than a mile from the police department."

Tanner turned on his signal and made a right.

"Academy Street?"

"I'm taking the scenic route." He moved down the street, frequently checking his mirror. A half minute later, the car followed. After two more turns, it was still behind him.

"Call 911, then hand me the phone."

He wouldn't head to the station. Otherwise the assailant would take off. Instead, he'd let the police come to them.

Kat did as he asked, then slid down in the seat as much as the belt would allow. Creases of concern marked the bridge of her nose, and her hands were curled into fists.

When the dispatcher came on, Tanner explained the situation and relayed what he knew about the vehicle, which wasn't much. Boxy, older model, lighter color. It was still too far back to identify the driver or even tell if someone occupied the passenger seat.

Before Tanner could finish his report, the car made a sudden left turn. He blew out a frustrated breath and jammed on his brakes. "He knows we're onto him."

After turning around in the parking lot of a local business, he went in pursuit. For the next ten minutes, he combed the streets of Bryson City. So did the officer who was dispatched. Neither had any success. The car had vanished.

He braked at a stop sign. "I'm sorry. I'd really hoped we'd catch him."

"Me, too."

"Let's get that police report made."

With her wide eyes and creases of worry lining her face, she looked like a lamb being led to slaughter.

His heart twisted. He couldn't help her. He didn't know any more than she did about what they would find.

And though he'd love to say something that would take away the desperation he sensed, he wouldn't lie to her.

Or give her reassurances he couldn't back up.

THREE

Kat opened her eyes and stretched. If not for the sun slanting in through the window, she'd still be dead to the world. Compared with her sleeping arrangements the prior night, the hospital bed was pure bliss.

She hadn't learned anything at the police station. She'd thought they'd feed her prints into the computer and all her information would pop up on the screen. That was just Hollywood. According to the officer, in real life those things took time.

So this morning, she was still Kat, with no history beyond about forty hours ago.

Last night, she'd slept hard enough to dream—random, disjointed images of intimidation and violence. Whether based on actual experiences or the product of something the doctors had put in her IV, she couldn't say. Analyzing what she'd seen required too much effort. Already it was shrouded in fog, slipping away as she tried to grasp it.

She reached for the control next to her and pressed a button. The back of her bed rose, giving her a much better view of the room. The bed next to her was empty. But she wasn't alone. Tanner occupied the padded chair in the corner. He was slouched down, his head propped up by one hand. She winced. That couldn't be comfortable.

His eyes opened and he grimaced as he lifted his head.

"Did you stay here all night?"

He kneaded his neck muscles. "Yeah."

"I thought you were leaving and coming back today."

"I was. When I stepped off the elevator, two guys were waiting to get on. I'm sure they were harmless. But as I walked to my truck, I got to thinking how easy it would be for someone to check rooms until they found you. Unless you're in the psych ward or some kind of critical care, people can pretty much walk right in." His jaw tightened, and a fierce sense of protectiveness entered his gaze. "I didn't bring you out of those woods to let someone pick you off in the hospital."

Her stomach fluttered. She didn't need her memory to know she probably hadn't encountered many guys like Tanner. "Thank you for everything. I'm going to find a way to repay you."

"Remember, I'm a cop. Serving and protecting people is my job."

"You haven't been on the clock the past two days."

"Doesn't matter. That need to protect is innate. It doesn't end when the shift does."

She released a sigh. If there was some guy waiting for her at home, she almost felt sorry for him. Tanner would be a hard act to follow.

He drew in a breath. "Just because we've managed to evade him, we can't assume you're out of danger. Someone's determined to see you dead."

"It would help if I could remember who. Or why."

The doctors had done a CT scan and an MRI, and

put her through a bunch of verbal and motor skill assessments. She had some slight bruising of the brain tissue, but no fractures, hemorrhaging or blood clots. The diagnosis so far was a concussion with retrograde amnesia, which meant she couldn't remember anything before the injury. She could've told them that without all the tests.

What she really wanted to know was when her memory was going to return. None of the doctors had had an answer.

Tanner cast a glance through the open doorway. "Looks like they're working on breakfast deliveries." He pushed himself to his feet. "I'll get myself something and be back."

She watched him leave the room, then picked up the television remote. Last night, they'd watched the news, hoping to see a story involving her or the creep who was after her. There'd been none.

The Bryson City Police Department hadn't been able to find anything, either. No one fitting her description was listed in the missing persons database. Apparently her absence hadn't triggered any concern, which probably meant she lived alone. If she had a job, she hoped her employer cared enough to ask questions instead of firing her for not showing up.

Movement drew her attention to the doorway, where a hospital employee wheeled a food cart into the room. "Good morning. Are you ready for breakfast?"

"I'm starved."

The lady set the tray on the rolling table, which Kat turned to position in front of her. When she removed the circular plastic cover, pleasant aromas drifted upward from a plate holding pancakes and a generous serving of scrambled eggs.

She'd just started eating when Tanner came into the room with his own breakfast. He'd done the same thing last night, gotten his meal to-go so he could eat with her. He folded back the top on the Styrofoam container and scooped up a forkful of scrambled eggs. "I never asked how you slept last night."

"Better than you did."

He twisted, stretching his back. "I'm really going to appreciate my comfortable bed."

"I'm sure you'll be glad to get home."

Home. The word was supposed to conjure up images of warmth, comfort and security. Instead, it was an abstract thought, holding no meaning. Cold seeped into her core. What if she never got her memory back? What if she had to face the future without any past?

One of her doctors walked into the room as she was finishing breakfast. "Good morning. Do you remember who I am?"

"Dr. Fischer, the neurologist."

He looked pleased with her answer. But the events *following* her fall weren't the problem. He shone a light in her eyes and repeated some of the same commands he'd given her yesterday. She followed his instructions with ease.

"You seem to be doing well except for the amnesia." He made some notes in the chart. "Have any memories surfaced since yesterday?"

"None." She'd told him about the one with the knife, leaving out the detail that she'd been the one wielding it.

"You cracked your head pretty good, so there's the

physical component, but you may have some dissociative amnesia, as well."

"What's that?"

"Amnesia triggered by emotional trauma. It's the mind's protective mechanism. When something is too painful to deal with, the brain boxes it up and tucks it away."

Great. His explanation made her sound crazy. Or weak. *Weak* bothered her more than *crazy.*

"Any idea how long you're keeping me?" Not that she was in a hurry to be discharged. With no money or credit cards, she'd likely find herself in a shelter. Or on the street.

"If you don't take a turn for the worse, probably tomorrow. I'd like to observe you one more day."

Good. One more day to figure out who she was and come up with a plan.

Shortly after the doctor left, Bryson City's Officer Munson walked into the room. He was the same one who'd taken their statements yesterday. When her gaze fell on the file folder he held, anticipation coursed through her. He must have learned something, or he wouldn't be in her hospital room, armed with whatever was in that folder.

Her excitement fizzled. Maybe he was there to arrest her.

He greeted her and Tanner, then held up the folder. "I'm here with what I hope is good news."

Okay, anything that could get her arrested wouldn't be good news.

He pulled the remaining empty chair up to her bedside and opened the folder. "Your name is Paige Tatem. Your last known address is in Atlanta."

"Paige Tatem." She said the name aloud. She'd thought once she found out who she was, it would give her a sense of stability. But *Paige* didn't feel any more like hers than the name Tanner had given her.

The officer frowned. "The name isn't familiar?"

"Not at all. What else do you know about me?" She was almost afraid to ask. The fact that he'd been able to identify her through her fingerprints meant one of two things: she'd held a job that required certain security procedures or she was a criminal.

"I don't have your juvie record, but from age eighteen to twenty-two, you kept the Orlando Police Department busy."

Her stomach drew into a knot. "How old am I now?"

"Twenty-eight."

"So for the past six years, I've stayed out of trouble." That had to count for something.

"Sort of. You spent five of those six years in Lowell Correctional Institution in Florida. So, you've stayed clean for a year."

She crossed her arms in front of her, suddenly feeling chilled. At least she'd done her time. But she'd rather the cop had made his visit while Tanner was out. She was curious to know what she'd done, but she wanted to keep her personal life private. Or maybe it was just Tanner's opinion that she cared about.

She shrugged off the reservations. "Dare I ask what I was in trouble for?" Once everything was over and she returned to her regular life, she'd never see Tanner again. So it shouldn't matter what he thought of her.

But it did.

The officer consulted his folder. "Let's see. Grand

theft, assault, battery, possession, breaking and enter-
ing, vandalism."

As he spoke, she slid a glance toward Tanner. His
expression was unreadable. He probably didn't shock
easily. In the course of his duties, he'd likely seen everything.

The officer flipped to the last page in the folder.
"Whatever happened inside, you must have decided
you didn't want to go back. In the past year, you haven't
even had a parking ticket."

So she'd been clean for a year. But trouble had found
her anyway.

"You have three known addresses. Two from your
arrest records are in Orlando. The most recent is what's
on file with the DMV in Atlanta." He handed her a sheet
of paper containing the addresses, along with dates for
each.

After closing the folder, he continued, "The cops in
those neighborhoods can probably give you details that
I don't have. They do pretty well keeping up with what's
happening on their beat." He rose and handed her a card.
"If there's anything I can do for you, let me know."

After he walked from the room, she sat in silence,
trying to digest everything. She hadn't been a good person. That had changed, though. Or she'd gotten smarter
and not been caught.

Finally, Tanner spoke. "Are you okay?"

"It's not what I wanted to hear, but I'm all right." She
studied him. "You don't seem surprised by the news."

"I had my suspicions. That tattoo on your arm is a
common gang symbol."

She looked at the inked design, then shrugged. "At
least I've already paid my dues, so I won't be leaving

in handcuffs." She forced a smile. "Now that I have a name and address, I need to find a way home."

Tanner moved closer to occupy the chair the officer had vacated. "That wouldn't be a good idea."

"I need to go back. It's the only way I'm going to learn what happened and who's after me."

"If you charge in there not knowing the situation, you'll get yourself killed."

"And if I bury my head in the sand and hole up somewhere else, I might never remember. You heard what Dr. Fischer said. Part of what I'm experiencing was induced by emotional trauma. I have to face it."

"You will. But let's do it without putting a target on your back. You have to assume this guy knows you. Even if you just stumbled onto something, since you don't have your ID, he probably does. That would mean he has everything he needs to track you down."

Tanner's words sent a chill through her. "What do you propose? As of tomorrow, I have nowhere to stay. With no money or credit cards, I can't even rent a cheap motel room." The shelter she'd thought about earlier was an option. But being stuck there indefinitely while she tried to figure out who she was sounded like as much fun as sleeping in the woods.

"I can put you up at my place."

She narrowed her eyes. No way was she touching that. "I'll take my chances on my own."

"You'll have your privacy. There's a one-room cabin behind my house. With a solid, locking door."

So he'd picked up on her trust issues. But she had valid reasons for her concern. People didn't just do things out of the kindness of their hearts. She couldn't

remember how she'd learned it, but favors carried ob-
ligations, which left one indebted.

Never a good place to be.

She crossed her arms. "So, you'll let me stay in your
cabin. In exchange for what?"

"Cleaning. I just closed on the place a few days ago
and my focus has been on the house. I haven't made
it to the cabin yet. Trust me, if you get it livable, *I'll*
owe *you*."

She pondered what he'd said. It was a business transaction. She'd do a deep cleaning. In exchange, he'd let
her stay there for free. That was an arrangement she
could do.

"All right." She held out her hand. When he shook
it, she gave a sharp nod.

"Deal."

Tanner eased to a stop in front of the ranch-style
house on 294, west of Murphy. As promised, Dr. Fischer
had kept Paige a second night. Today, he'd released her
only after Tanner had promised to care for her and get
her to her follow-up appointment next week.

He killed the engine. "I'll show you your temporary
digs and you can get your stuff situated."

She slid from the truck, a Walmart bag in each hand.
They'd stopped on their way in to Murphy. He'd bought
her the bare necessities: two pairs of jeans, a pair of san-
dals to give her a lighter option than her hiking boots,
and three T-shirts so they could do laundry only twice a
week. Even then he'd had to twist her arm. She'd finally
agreed when he'd promised to keep track of everything
and let her pay him back once she could return home.

He led her to the porch, holding his own bags. While

she'd chosen her items, he'd picked up groceries. "The cabin's in the back, tucked away in the woods."

He'd probably feel better if he could see it from the house. But it made a great hideout. He wouldn't have known it was there himself if the sellers hadn't told him.

Although she'd be there alone, she wouldn't be cut off. He'd also tossed a throwaway phone into the cart. If she needed anything, he'd be a phone call away. No matter the hour, his ringtone would bring him instantly awake.

He'd always been a light sleeper. When he'd been small, he'd never known when the next fight was going to erupt. Or, once it did, whether it would stay in his mom's room or grow to involve him and his sister. In the group homes, he'd never known when he might wake up with his toenails painted or his head shaved. By the time he was an adult, sleeping with one eye open had become second nature.

He twisted his key in the lock and swung open the front door. "Welcome."

She stepped inside with the barest hint of a limp. She'd left the hospital with a prescription for some pain meds but refused to let him fill it. She'd insisted the headache had retreated to a dull throb and the sprained ankle was healed except for some slight tenderness. Of course, she wasn't likely to tell him otherwise. If there was anything he'd learned about Paige, it was that she bore life's hardships without complaint.

He closed the door behind them. "I've wrestled most of the disorder into submission."

"For someone who just moved a few days ago, this is pretty amazing. You must be a neat freak."

He smiled. "I've been accused of that before." It

had been the one area of control in a life where he'd otherwise had none.

He led her past the leather sectional sofa and entertainment center toward the kitchen. Two boxes still sat against the wall, framed pictures, photo albums and other memorabilia inside. Soon he'd get around to displaying the items from his college days and the souvenirs he'd acquired during his travels.

Dealing with the photo albums would take longer. Some of the pictures would have to go. Kevin occupied too many of them. So did Brittney, his ex-fiancée.

He laid the groceries on the counter, then backtracked to the hall. After loading up on sheets, pillowcases, towels and washcloths, he removed a flashlight from the kitchen drawer. Once the sun went down, the path through the woods would be pitch-black.

"I'd rather you not use this." He held up the flashlight. "If you need to come to the house after dark, call me. I'll have that phone activated before you go to bed tonight."

After crossing the small backyard, Tanner stepped into the woods with Paige right behind him. The deciduous trees were still acquiring their new leaves, but evergreens shielded the cabin from view.

A half minute later, it stood in front of them, measuring about fifteen by fifteen with a porch spanning its front. In the corner sat a rocker, left behind by the prior owner.

A smile climbed up Paige's cheeks. "This is cute."

He had to agree. It needed a coat or two of stain and some weather seal, but it would make a great vacation cottage.

When he pushed the door open, it creaked on its

hinges, and a musty scent assaulted him. Sunlight slanted in through one dirty window, illuminating the airborne dust in its path. A rug covered a portion of the scratched hardwood floor, a couch and stuffed chairs at three of its edges. The kitchen occupied one rear corner, a daybed and chest of drawers the other. One closed door led to a bathroom, the other to a closet.

"It's small, but once it's cleaned up, I think it'll be comfortable."

"It's wonderful." She flashed him another smile. "If you give me some cleaning supplies, I'll have it shaped up in no time. Then you'll have to find something else for me to earn my keep."

"How good are you at cooking?"

"I'm not sure. I bet it would come back, though."

"I might take you up on that." He headed toward the door. "I'm going to give you time to get settled and get some rest while I activate the phone." Then they'd be heading to Colton's.

Now that he was living in Murphy, activities with his friends were going to be a regular occurrence. Both Colton and Bryce lived nearby, Bryce on Ranger Road a mile or so away, and Colton on Hilltop Road, the next street east. Tonight's gathering, though, would be as much brainstorming as socializing.

Bryson City PD was getting with the proper authorities to investigate the incidents in the woods. By now, they'd probably already combed them. But it wouldn't hurt for Tanner and his friends to put their heads together. Bryce's background was law enforcement, too—Cherokee County sheriff—and Colton was a district attorney.

He returned to the cabin thirty minutes later, with

the phone in one hand and two folded bills in the other. Paige had changed the bed and left the dirty linens in a pile by the door. Her clothing purchases were either tucked away in the closet in the corner or the chest of drawers nearby.

He held out the phone. "For you."

"Thank you. Add this to my list of expenses. I'm paying you back."

Accepting charity obviously bothered her. She struck him as someone used to taking care of herself. Maybe she'd grown up that way. Maybe the adults in her life had let her down, and she'd had no one she could depend on but herself. He could relate.

He unfolded the bills, a twenty and a ten. "This is for you, too."

Instead of taking them, she frowned down at them. "What for?"

"Just to hang on to. You shouldn't need them, since you'll be with me, but I think you'll feel better not walking around broke." He couldn't do anything about her missing memory, but maybe the small gesture would make her feel less helpless, a little more in control.

She hesitated, brows raised. Suspicion gave way to surprise, then appreciation. "Thank you." She reached for the bills. "That's really sweet of you."

He extended a hand toward the door, palm up. "Ready to go? Burgers are waiting."

When they arrived at Colton's house, the aroma of grilling meat called to him as soon as he got out of the truck, and he headed around the side of the house. Colton and Bryce stood at the grill. Smoke puffed from the vent holes and rose upward. Colton's wife, Mandy, would be inside, preparing condiments and whatever would accompany the burgers. Little Liam was probably having some serious one-on-one time with his pacifier.

Colton turned, and an easy smile spread across his face. "You must be Paige." He held out a hand. "Colton Gale. Glad you're joining us."

As Paige accepted the handshake, Colton cast a glance at Tanner. "If this guy gives you any problems, let us know."

The shove Colton gave him would have knocked him off balance a few years ago. As teenagers, it was Kevin who'd always been big enough no one would mess with him. Tanner and Colton had had to grow into their size.

Now, at five foot ten, Tanner was still several inches shorter than either of his friends. But lots of good eating and countless hours pumping iron had given him the bulk he'd dreamed of as a scrawny adolescent.

Soon they were all spread throughout the living room, enjoying burgers, baked beans, chips and potato salad. Except Liam, who was sitting on Mandy's lap, allowing her to spoon some kind of green goo into his mouth. A wooden TV tray sat in front of each of the adults, set with extra napkins and the full complement of plastic utensils. Mandy's presence brought a sense of civility to their gatherings.

It also brought a sense of home. Family. Stability. Colton had everything that mattered.

Bryce took a bite of burger, then talked around it. "Any new developments?"

Tanner had already filled them in on the basics. "Yesterday, Swain County detectives combed the area. All they recovered were two canteens filled with water. Prints haven't come back yet."

Colton's gaze shifted to Paige. "I take it you still have no memory of what happened?"

Paige shook her head, and Tanner continued, "The only memory she's had is the one I told you about yesterday."

Colton's brow creased. "Maybe she was hiking, came upon the scene, and the guy with the knife proceeded to slit the other guy's throat. He knows she can identify him."

Paige shook her head. "What I remembered didn't happen in the woods. There was concrete at the guy's back, like a sidewalk."

Bryce laid down his burger. "Try to recall the scene."

She sat motionless, brows drawn together. Finally, she shook her head. "I see the guy and the concrete on either side of him. Nothing beyond that."

Colton nodded. "Anything you can tell us about the hand holding the knife?"

She fiddled with her napkin and her eyes dipped to her plate. "No."

Tanner tensed. She was hiding something. If she had a suspicion about the identity of the killer, why would she keep that from them? Maybe she was afraid. Or maybe she was protecting someone.

He shot Colton and Bryce a quick glance. They both watched Paige, eyes alert but narrowed. They'd seen it, too. When he got her alone, he'd demand an explanation.

"Okay," Colton said. "Let's say you witnessed a murder…somewhere. Why would you head off to hike the Appalachian Trail knowing someone's after you?"

Bryce shrugged. "Maybe she didn't go willingly. Maybe the killer took her, planning to march her into the woods and kill her, but she managed to get away."

Tanner nodded slowly. "What triggered the other memory was my holding up my knife. We need more triggers."

Paige lifted a brow. "What do you suggest?"

"You guys got addresses from the cop," Bryce said. "Why don't you visit the Atlanta one?"

Tanner frowned. "Not without knowing what we're walking into. Even with police protection, it could be dangerous. I'd rather her see what she can find online."

Paige nodded. "I was thinking the same thing. I'd like to Google my name and also see what comes up for the addresses Officer Munson gave me."

"I agree," said Bryce. "It's better to not go home until you figure this out."

Eventually, Mandy put Liam to bed, then returned to sit near Paige. The conversation grew more lighthearted. Soon they were reminiscing, each event embellished from what Tanner remembered.

As the evening wore on, the stories became more outrageous and entertaining. Kevin figured prominently in every one. Years ago, Tanner's stocky friend had been his hero, the one who'd kept the bullies at bay. Tanner owed him a lot. He'd have been willing to give him almost anything.

Except his fiancée.

Betrayal was the pits. Especially when it came from the closest of friends.

Sometime later, Tanner left with Paige, promising to keep his buddies apprised of any new developments. No matter what happened, they'd have his back. He pulled onto 64 and headed toward home. His plan was to pin Paige down and demand some answers. But maybe he should give her a day or two to feel she could trust him.

Actually, a day or two was overly optimistic. Although she was appreciative, she was guarded. Maybe her guard being up was a protective mechanism and once she got her memory back, she'd relax. Or maybe life had been so cruel that keeping everyone shut out was her usual modus operandi.

He hoped it was the former. Everyone needed someone close enough to let past those invisible walls. For him, it was Colton and Bryce. He'd trust either of them with his life. Of course, he'd trusted Kevin, too. And look where that had gotten him.

"You three guys seem close." Paige's words interrupted his thoughts.

"We are. Colton and I were thirteen when we landed in the same group home. We stayed together till age fifteen. Then he got adopted."

"You never did?"

"Nope. Stayed in the system till I aged out."

"That makes me sad." She looked over at him. "That probably doesn't make sense, considering that my past may be no different from yours."

"Maybe that's why it makes you sad."

Although Colton had been about to burst with the news that a family wanted him, Tanner hadn't shared that excitement. It had been Kevin and Colton who'd made his years in the group home bearable. They'd become his replacement family, and he'd lost one of them.

As an adult, he was happy Colton had gotten parents who loved him. And he was happy for the life Colton now had, with a woman who adored him and a little mini-Colton.

Happy and often envious.

"Your mom and dad…" She glanced over at him. "I'm sorry. That's none of my business."

"It's all right. I never knew my dad. My mom was killed by an angry boyfriend."

"That's awful."

It was. But he sort of understood. Although his mom didn't deserve to die, it was her own bad choices that had led to it. Not Teri, though. His sweet sister was innocent.

"Did Bryce grow up in foster care, too?"

"No. Colton and I got connected up with him about eight years ago."

Until then they'd been a threesome—he and Kevin and Colton—adventurers in search of the next challenge. Then Bryce joined them, and they became four.

After Mandy came along, Colton's priorities shifted. Now his evenings were occupied with baby bottles and burp cloths instead of backpacking and rafting plans. And they'd all severed ties with Kevin.

If there was one constant Tanner had learned over the years, it was that things constantly changed.

As Tanner pulled into his driveway, his headlights swept the front of the house. He jammed on the brakes, a block of ice settling in his gut.

"What's wrong?"

"The front door's ajar."

Paige gasped. "Someone broke in?"

Without responding, he backed from the drive. A killer could be waiting. Once he'd driven to where 294 met the four-lane, he dialed 911 and filled the dispatcher in on their situation. It didn't take long for a unit to arrive. He followed the officer back to the house, then allowed him to lead the way inside.

As Tanner stepped past the splintered doorjamb with Paige, he glanced around the living room. Everything had been pulled from the entertainment center shelves. Couch cushions were stewed around the room, with the contents of the two boxes he'd yet to unpack tossed into the mess.

While Paige waited in the living room, he inspected the rest of the house. Every other room was in the same condition. He moved from his bedroom into the hall where the officer stood.

"Is anything missing?"

"Not that I can tell." He wouldn't know for sure until he got everything put away. At least his electronics appeared undisturbed. His laptop sat on the kitchen table, and the TV and DVD player still occupied their slots in the entertainment center.

The officer moved down the hall toward the living room. "I'll dust for prints, if you'd like. Any idea what they were looking for?"

"Not a clue." At least *he* didn't know. If Paige did, she hadn't volunteered any information.

When the officer exited through the front door, Tanner looked at Paige. She was sitting on the arm of the couch, staring up at him with wide eyes. Her face wasn't much darker than the cream-colored T-shirt she wore.

His heart twisted. "You can't stay here."

"I know." She swallowed hard, her throat working with the action. "This is my fault. I'm so sorry."

"That's not what I mean. Whoever's after you knows you were with me, and he found me." He shouldn't have been so quick to trade in the Kentucky driver's license and tag for North Carolina ones. For someone with the right connections, locating his address would be easy.

But procrastination wasn't in his vocabulary. Taking care of business at the earliest possible moment made him feel more in control.

He crossed his arms. "I'm taking you to the Hampton Inn in town."

"For how long?" She rose from her perch, arms spread, palms up. "I don't know my financial situation. What if I can't pay for it?"

"Only until we figure out safe accommodations."

"Maybe he didn't find the cabin."

The front door opened and the officer entered, cutting off any further argument. He held up the kit. "I'll try to lift some prints."

While he set about dusting the front door, Tanner leaned against the entertainment center. "You know, this changes everything."

"How?"

"We thought you witnessed a murder. Now it looks like you have something someone wants."

"I don't have anything except that wooden box. I don't think anyone would try to kill me for that, even if the joints were still there."

"Apparently you had something at one point. Maybe when he was closing in on you, you hid it, hoping to buy yourself some time."

"What?"

"No idea. If you could remember the *where*, maybe we could find the *what*."

"I don't even remember having anything. How am I supposed to figure out where I put it?"

"We go back to the woods."

The rest of the color drained from her face, but she didn't argue.

"We'll take Bryce with us. He and I will be armed. The only way we're going to solve this is for you to regain your memory. Maybe the best way to do that is to return to where you lost it."

He stepped forward to put a hand on her shoulder.

"We need to find whatever you had. Because someone wants it bad enough to kill you to get it."

FOUR

Paige bolted upright with a gasp, her heart beating out a staccato rhythm. The faintest hint of light seeped in around the cabin's curtains. Since there'd been no moon the past two nights, the soft glow had to be the first promise of sunrise. *Thank the Lord.*

She squeezed her eyes shut, but the action did nothing to erase the image etched into her mind.

A young man. Dark eyes wide, shining with a desperate plea.

One that was ignored.

The sharp crack of gunfire, the sudden hole in his forehead. The flash of recognition in his eyes, then horror, as death captured and held him in its unrelenting grip.

The scene played out in full color, at point-blank range.

As if she was the one who'd fired the shot.

Had she killed him in self-defense? Or was she a murderer?

She thrust back the covers and swung her legs over the edge of the bed. Another memory she wouldn't share with Tanner. At least not the details.

Last night, when Colton had asked if she could tell them anything about the hand holding the knife, she'd said no. Tanner had looked at her with suspicion. Colton and Bryce had, too.

What she'd said was true. She *couldn't* tell them. Tanner and Bryce were cops. If either of them suspected she'd killed someone, they'd have to turn her in. She couldn't let that happen. With no memory, she was defenseless.

She reached for the phone to check the time. It lay on the small chest of drawers next to the bed, the folded bills Tanner had given her beneath it.

His taking her clothes shopping had meant a lot. So had buying the phone. But giving her the thirty dollars had just about disarmed her. He'd wanted to offer her a sliver of security in a world where she'd completely lost her footing. The gesture had made her go all gooey inside.

She pressed a button and the phone lit up—6:22 a.m. Tanner would arrive in less than an hour to escort her to breakfast.

It had been a short night for both of them. As soon as the officer had finished his investigation, Tanner had temporarily secured his front door, planning to have someone make permanent repairs today. Even though the cabin was undisturbed, she'd had to fight him about sleeping there. He was afraid her pursuer would come back.

She had the same fear. But she was more afraid of racking up a debt she couldn't pay. She'd promised to reimburse Tanner when she could get to her money. That was assuming she had some. The information Bryson

City provided didn't include employment. They hadn't even located next of kin.

If she *was* gainfully employed, she probably wouldn't be by the time she could return home. Everything would hinge on whether she'd stashed anything away in savings.

When she finished dressing, she picked up the wooden box and slid her fingers over its varnished surface. A cold hollowness settled in her core, and her chest tightened around it. She couldn't remember the specifics, but the box had bad memories associated with it. Disappointment and anger. A sense of betrayal.

Finally, she laid it aside. It was no use. Other than a few vague emotions, she wasn't getting anywhere. Maybe once she made it to the woods, it would come back to her.

After lacing her hiking boots, she slid the phone into her pocket. When she picked up the folded bills, something stirred. She stared down at what she held. It was money. What could be more generic than that? But the memory that hovered just out of reach was personal. Someone had stolen from her. Someone she trusted.

What? Had everyone betrayed her? Or did those memories just happen to be closest to the surface?

The factory-set ringtone sounded, and she pulled the phone from her pocket. When she put it to her ear, Tanner's liquid-smooth voice sent warmth surging through her chest.

"Are you up?"

"Have been for a while. Apparently I'm an early riser." At least when nightmares plagued her.

"Good. I just put breakfast in the oven. I'll walk you over shortly."

That warmth was still there as she disconnected the call. When it came to kindness and compassion, Tanner had a double dose. With those piercing green eyes, casually tousled hair and powerful body, he wasn't bad to look at, either.

She scolded herself. She wasn't going to be attracted to her rescuer. Okay, maybe she was. But she wouldn't let what she felt go any further than appreciation and gratitude.

She held out her left hand and studied the lighter band of skin that circled her ring finger. She'd apparently worn the ring for some time. And removed it recently. Was she divorced? In the process? Maybe she had kids.

A cold wave of dread crashed over her. Surely if she had children, that knowledge would stay with her regardless of the memory loss. And there would be physical signs.

A quick inspection silenced the alarms. Her stomach was flat and toned, abdominal muscles hard beneath skin devoid of stretch marks. It wasn't proof positive, but it made the possibility that she'd left little ones behind a lot less likely.

Fifteen minutes later, she was sitting at Tanner's kitchen table, enjoying a plateful of eggs, potatoes and ham, baked together with ingredients that probably included sour cream and cheese. In addition to making breakfast, he'd managed to wrestle at least the front rooms back into order.

Soon a firm knock reverberated through the house. After checking the peephole, Tanner swung open the front door. Bryce stood on the porch wearing a light windbreaker. The bulge at his left hip was reassuring. Tanner was armed, too.

"All clear?"

Bryce nodded. "I drove up 294, then doubled back. I even ventured into your woods, looking for signs anyone had been there."

"And?"

"Nothing."

Tanner picked up a backpack he'd filled earlier and ushered her through the open door. The men had discussed making the trip in Bryce's Sorento, since it would be less recognizable than the Silverado. Then they'd decided that, if the killer was going to strike, they'd rather it be when they were both armed and prepared.

Paige reached for the door handle. "I'll take the backseat." She'd feel safer there, behind the tinted windows, ready to release the belt and hit the floorboard at a moment's notice.

After leaving Murphy and passing through Andrews, 74 became an unending series of S curves, the highway following the tortuous course of the Nantahala River. When they finally arrived at the Outdoor Center, the parking lot was empty. At a quarter till nine on an April morning, it wasn't open yet. Behind them was another building that housed restrooms and a concession area, also closed. Come summer, when the rafting business exploded, everything would probably be bustling with activity.

Bryce handed Tanner a pen and trail map, apparently retrieved from his shirt pocket. "See if you can figure out where you found Paige."

She leaned forward and watched Tanner trace the

winding blue line that represented the Nantahala River. He veered into the variegated brown-and-green area and drew a circle. "I think it was somewhere around here."

Bryce pointed and the map and turned to her. "Since this is the stretch of the trail that comes closest to that point, you most likely veered off here."

Once out of the vehicle, they circled the building and followed signs to the trail, Bryce leading, Tanner in the rear. Cocooned between two strong men, she almost felt safe. The pistols they wore didn't hurt, either.

The narrow trail was steep and rocky, and a heavy rain had left some areas slick. She kept her eyes downward to avoid stumbling. Soon her heart rate was well into its target zone, and her thigh muscles burned. Tanner crunched along behind her, sounding as winded as she was.

Bryce stopped under a huge outcropping of rock and turned to face them. "We've probably got a six-mile walk, one way." He sucked in a couple of deep breaths. "Are you up for it?"

The question was for her, not Tanner. Something flared inside. She was a woman, but she was no dainty flower. He should be able to tell that by looking at her. When his eyes dipped to her foot, she snapped her mouth shut, the flame doused.

"I plan to give you guys a run for your money. My ankle's almost back to normal." She had no pain unless she twisted her foot inward. Tanner had offered her an elastic bandage, but the high-top hiking boots did the job.

Bryce nodded. "Then we'll keep going."

They climbed several more slopes, with short downhill reprieves between. As they moved farther from the

Nantahala, the *shh* of the river gradually faded, then disappeared altogether.

"Anything familiar?" Tanner's voice came from close behind her.

"Nothing. But based on where you found me, I'm guessing I've hiked this before." Probably more than once, judging from how well she was keeping up with the men.

For the next three hours, they hiked up one slope and down the next, following the mountain ridges. With her knowledge of wild plants, she'd suspected she was an avid hiker. Now she understood why. Interspersed with evergreens, hardwoods rose skyward, limbs bursting with new spring growth. The occasional wild azalea bloomed brilliant orange, and another bush whose name hovered just out of reach dotted the landscape with bursts of pink.

So far, they'd encountered only three people: a man and woman hiking together and a guy going solo. All carried large packs, with sleeping mats folded accordion-style and tied to the outside.

Finally, Tanner stopped. "What do you say we eat lunch?" He was now in the lead, he and Bryce having swapped places throughout the course of the morning. Regardless of their position, they'd always kept her in the middle.

After shedding their backpacks, Tanner distributed peanut butter sandwiches, and Bryce contributed apples, stick cheese and chips. She didn't have a pack. Supposedly neither Bryce nor Tanner had one they could lend her. A third pack probably wasn't as hard to locate as they let on.

Tanner bit into his sandwich, then spread out the map with his free hand.

Paige leaned toward it. "So, where are we?"

"Looks like this ridge here."

She nodded. Tanner's circled area was ahead and to the left. Soon they would veer off and trek through the woods. In July or August, undergrowth would probably have impeded their way. Mid-April wasn't bad.

After they gathered up their trash, they set out again, studying the flora on the left side of the trail. Nothing appeared broken or trampled down. If dead leaves had been kicked aside or footprints left, the storm that had blown through in the early-morning hours had washed them away.

Bryce stepped off the trail and picked his way down the steep slope, grasping branches for support. Paige followed. Limbs and twigs snapped behind her, sounds of Tanner following. She froze and closed her eyes.

A memory stirred. No, not a memory. An emotion. Desperation. Terror.

"Are you all right?"

She started at Tanner's voice so close to her ear.

"I'm sorry." He squeezed her shoulders. "I didn't mean to startle you."

His hands traveled down her arms and back up again, the action calming. She fought the urge to lean into him, the desire for the comfort and security he offered warring with an innate sense of independence.

"Did you remember something?" The soothing timbre of his voice sent a wave of goose bumps over her.

"I think so." She drew in a shaky breath. Bryce had stopped walking and stood watching them. "I remember running, like I was being chased."

"Do you remember who was chasing you?"

She shook her head.

"That's all right. It's a start."

When they began walking again, the men traded places once more, putting Tanner in the lead. His head pivoted back and forth as he studied their surroundings. Then he veered off to the right and increased his pace. About fifty feet away, a large boulder protruded from the downward slope, its outer edge forming a steep drop-off. Paige's pulse picked up.

When Tanner reached it, he rested one hand against the rock face. "This is where I found Paige." The statement was for Bryce. She didn't need it. Whatever happened with her other memories, those initial moments of terror on first awakening would stay with her the rest of her life.

Bryce drew to a stop next to her. "Any hints about how you ended up here?"

She followed the upward slope with her eyes. She'd likely lost her footing and tumbled downward, head over heels, until she'd landed unconscious behind the boulder. There were telltale signs the storms hadn't swept away, if one was looking—cracked and broken twigs on the sparse underbrush clinging to the side of the slope.

"It looks like I tumbled down that incline, but the first thing I remember is waking up with Tanner there."

Tanner nodded. "Let's retrace your steps and see if you can remember what you were running from."

She headed up the slope, stopping regularly to close her eyes and search her memory. Images drifted on the fringes of her consciousness, shrouded in fog. Whenever she tried to grasp one, it retreated further, leaving nothing but swirling mist.

When they finally reached the trail, she shook her head. "Nothing. I'm sorry."

"You said detectives found two canteens." Bryce's eyes were on Tanner. "Let's assume they belong to Paige."

Tanner nodded. "Both were full. If they were hers, she apparently left the trail to get water. On her way back, someone chased her, and she dropped them."

Bryce gave a sharp dip of his head. "Sounds logical. Hand me the map."

Tanner complied, then stood next to Bryce as he studied it. Thin blue ribbons wove through the landscape. Bryce pointed. "This looks like the nearest water source."

Bryce led the way this time, and soon the trickle of water drifted to them on the soft breeze.

Paige walked down the slope to the creek and stood at its edge. She'd probably been in this very spot, or somewhere close, days earlier. Frustration built inside. Why couldn't she remember?

She drew in a cleansing breath and released it slowly. Nothing was going to happen if she tried to force it. She eased into a squat and closed her eyes. The sounds of the woods surrounded her, the calls of wrens and other birds punctuating the steadier sounds of trickling water and rustling leaves. She mimed removing the lid from a canteen and dipping it into the cool water. There was something soothing in the action, the sense of the familiar. She'd done this. More than once, and recently.

She rose and looked around. Where had she gone after getting water? "I remember filling canteens. But that's all." She'd pried open a brief window in time, but the events surrounding it were still held under lock and key.

She heaved a sigh. Today's trek had been a waste of time. She plodded up the slope, Tanner next to her, Bryce bringing up the rear. When she reached the trail, she turned toward them, an apology ready on her lips.

But Tanner wasn't looking at her. He was looking farther up the trail. They stood on a peak, the forest stretched out around them. Ahead and to the right, birds moved in a slow circle.

Vultures.

Something dark fluttered through her.

"We should check it out." Bryce had seen it, too.

They followed the trail north, verifying their position at each peak. Finally, Tanner pointed down the slope. "Right over there."

Paige swallowed hard. A couple hundred feet away, vultures continued to circle, their big black wings glistening in the midafternoon sun. She followed Tanner off the trail, the diagonal trek making the slope a little less steep.

A few minutes later, the ground rose in a steady incline. The breeze shifted, carrying the faint scent of death. Dread trickled through her, the sense of gloom as black as the birds she could no longer see but knew circled overhead.

She shook off the sensation. It was probably an animal. A deer. Maybe a dead bear. But no matter how hard she tried to reason away the uneasiness, it remained.

She moved forward, plodding through briars, around trees and over rocks. The breeze shifted again, gagging her with the stench of rotting flesh.

An image shimmered into focus, the man with terror-filled eyes.

Her step faltered and one knee buckled. Whatever lay ahead of them, it was no animal. It was a man.

If she had to guess, she'd say it was the man from her dream.

Tanner pressed a hand over his mouth and nose, but the foul odor seeped between his fingers anyway, filling his lungs and sinuses. He knew what they'd find. He'd smelled decay enough times to recognize the scent. Rats and other small animals numerous times. Human, only twice. Most of the bodies he encountered in his line of work were discovered long before reaching the decay stage.

But Paige probably didn't face death on a regular basis. She didn't need to see this.

He stopped walking. "One of us should stay here with Paige while the other sees what's there."

"No." Paige gripped his arm. "I'm sure I've already seen whatever we're going to find."

Tanner nodded. What happened there was probably the event that triggered the dissociative amnesia. Revisiting it could bring back her entire memory. Or cause a meltdown.

"Are you sure? We can stay here and let Bryce investigate."

"I need to do this."

Tanner began moving again, staying next to her as they walked. He resisted the urge to wrap an arm around her. But if she needed to lean on him, he'd be ready.

"Look over there."

Bryce's words cut into his thoughts. Some distance to

their right, objects littered the ground. Two backpacks lay nearby, one large and one small. They hurried in that direction, and Paige squatted in front of the larger pack.

Tanner touched the arm she extended. "Don't disturb anything."

She withdrew her hand, eyes still on the items slung around—protein bars, packets of dried fruit, trail mix, crackers, cans of tuna…and a pair of jeans and several tanks that looked suspiciously close to her size.

"This is mine. I feel a sense of ownership without an actual memory."

So, if the larger pack belonged to Paige, who did the other one belong to? Was she hiking with another woman?

The pack lay about ten feet away, with T-shirts, jeans and cigarette packs scattered around it. Apparently Paige had carried all the food. If there was a wallet with either pack, it was hidden in the bottom or mixed among the clothing. Same with cell phones. They'd leave those questions for the crime scene unit.

Meanwhile, there was a body nearby. Judging from the smell, it was close. They'd locate it, then find cell service and report everything.

Tanner took Paige's hand and headed up the slope after Bryce. At the top, they stopped. The ground fell away, a long downward descent. Water trickled in a meandering path at its bottom.

But it wasn't the small mountain creek that snagged Tanner's gaze. It was the dozen or so birds clustered together, vying for the best position. One jeans-clad leg protruded from behind a downed tree, the rest of the body hidden by the plants growing at the stream's edge.

Bryce made his way down the slope at a slow jog

and looked back at them, his face a grimace of disgust. "It's bad. You don't want to see this."

Tanner put a hand on Paige's shoulder. "Trust me, these kinds of images can haunt you for a long time." *Some never go away.*

"It's important that I face this."

He gave her shoulder a squeeze. "It won't serve any purpose. Let the police handle it."

Paige stiffened, then shrugged away his hand. "I have to do this."

He understood. If their roles were reversed, he'd do whatever he had to do to restore those neural pathways.

At the creek's edge, Paige skidded to a stop so suddenly he almost bumped into her. A man lay with his face submerged, torso and limbs positioned awkwardly on the bank as if he'd tumbled to his death.

But drowning wasn't what had killed him. His hair was matted to the back of his head, bits of flesh, dried blood and bone fragments clinging to it. In the center was a jagged hole. He'd likely been shot through the forehead at point-blank range.

Paige swayed beside him. Two tears had found their way between her tightly closed eyelids and trickled down her cheeks. All the color had drained from her face, and she'd bitten down on her lower lip so hard she was sure to draw blood.

He wrapped both arms around her and held her against him. Maybe later she wouldn't appreciate it, but right now, he was going with his gut. And his gut said she needed him.

He'd guessed right. Instead of stiffening, her body went almost limp in his arms. Those invisible walls had crumbled. Her sudden dependence stirred something inside, a longing he hadn't known he had. He'd be there for her as long as she needed him.

When she finally pulled away, he led her a few yards upstream and eased her to the ground with him. "Are you all right?"

She clasped both arms around her knees and rocked back and forth. "We were together."

"Who is he?"

She wiped her eyes and shook her head. "I don't know. But I witnessed something terrible here, and I feel this gut-wrenching sense of loss. He was someone I cared about."

Bryce approached, and Tanner shook his head. "She knew him but doesn't remember who he is."

He glanced at Paige. She'd stopped rocking, but her eyes held a vacancy that was disturbing. He put an arm around her again, and she leaned against his side, her head resting on his chest. If Bryce questioned their closeness, he chose to keep it to himself.

Since meeting Bryce eight years ago, Tanner had never known him to be in a serious relationship. He dated some but always kept it casual. Although Bryce hadn't provided details, Tanner had pieced together a likely scenario from the snippets his friend *had* provided. He'd apparently never forgotten the one who'd gotten away. Or the girl he'd stupidly let go.

That wasn't Tanner's situation. His life was more a series of missteps along a continual quest for something that remained out of reach. Colton had found it. He and Bryce never had. Maybe they never would.

Bryce removed his phone from his pocket, then frowned at the screen. "We need to find a signal and get this reported. But someone should stay to preserve the scene."

Tanner nodded. "Go back to a high point on the trail and make that call. I'll stay here with Paige."

"No." Paige pushed herself to her feet. "I need to walk."

Tanner straightened with her. Sitting still while everything inside screamed for escape was its own kind of torture. When Colton had left the group home with his new family, Tanner had circled the neighborhood day after day. While he kicked sticks and soda cans and anything else in his path, he railed against the Gales for taking his buddy, against Colton for leaving and against God, who was supposed to love him but had always turned a blind eye to his suffering. He'd since forgiven the Gales and no longer blamed Colton. But God was still on his do-not-call list.

When he and Paige arrived at the trail, he backtracked to the nearest peak and checked his phone. Two bars. He placed the call, relaying what they'd found and describing the location as best he could.

Now they'd have to wait. A unit could be at the Nantahala Outdoor Center in a matter of minutes. But it would take time for detectives to reach them on the trail.

Paige sank onto a boulder. "Why didn't the police find him earlier, before the birds…" Her voice was paper-thin.

"He was probably outside the search perimeter and the vultures hadn't discovered him yet. This is farther north and on the opposite side of the trail from where you fell and where they found the canteens."

By the time Swain County officers arrived, the sun had sunk to rest on the treetops. He and Paige led the detectives to where Bryce waited near the packs. After answering a series of questions, the three of them left the law enforcement personnel to their business.

Daylight turned to dusk, then darkness, as they made their trek back, forcing them to finish via the flashlight apps on their phones.

At the truck, Bryce reached for the back-passenger door. "Sit up front with Tanner this time. I'll take the back." Paige nodded. Once they'd all settled inside, Bryce continued, "You guys should come and stay with me."

Tanner cranked the truck, casting him a glance over one shoulder. "When are your parents arriving?"

Bryce flinched. "Tomorrow evening, but they won't mind staying in their motor home." They'd spent the past several months touring the country, newly retired. Every few weeks they'd show up at Bryce's for a visit before heading out again.

Paige crossed her arms. "I refuse to put anyone else in danger."

"Then let me get you a hotel room." Even as he said the words, Tanner knew his plea was pointless.

"I won't rack up bills I can't pay."

He pulled onto 19 and headed toward home. "Let's go to Bryce's tonight. Tomorrow we'll come up with a better plan." Maybe by then, he could talk some sense into her and get her checked into a hotel.

When Tanner pulled into his driveway, Paige sat with her head resting against the passenger-side window, eyes closed. He gave her a gentle shake. "We're here." They'd grab some personal items, then follow Bryce home.

Tanner glanced around, then stepped from the truck

while Bryce exited the other side. As he closed the door, a wave of uneasiness washed over him, leaving goose bumps in its wake. All senses shot to full alert. Something moved in his peripheral vision, and he raised an arm in defense. A long cylindrical object grazed his forearm before connecting with the side of his head.

Pain shot through his temple, exploding in a flash of light. Stars twinkled against the black curtain closing over his vision, and he slumped against the truck.

A muffled scream penetrated the fog surrounding him. Then shouts. Then silence. His eyes fell shut and he slid down the side of the truck. A hand gripped his shoulder.

"Are you all right?"

Bryce's voice sounded far away, but when Tanner forced his eyes open, his friend was leaning over him.

Tanner blinked several times. "Did you see anything?"

"Someone ran from behind a tree and whacked you upside the head with a baseball bat. I chased him, but he disappeared into the woods."

Tanner shook his head, trying to clear it. Bryce chased the attacker? When? "We need to call the police."

"I already did."

Okay, Bryce chased the attacker *and* called the police. Tanner blinked again. He'd been out of it longer than he'd thought.

He pulled himself up, using the side mirror for support, and looked around. He and Bryce were alone. His heart almost stopped. "Where's Paige?"

"On the floorboard of your truck. I told her to stay out of sight. I'm sure the attacker's gone, but I need to get you both inside."

Tanner expelled a pent-up breath. Paige was safe.

The assailant probably hadn't noticed Bryce sitting in the backseat. If Bryce hadn't been there... He pushed the thought from his mind.

When he opened the driver's-side door, light flooded the interior of the truck. Paige looked up with fear-filled eyes. "Are you okay?"

"Ask me tomorrow. Right now, I think my brain is going to explode." Actually, his forearm hurt, too. The bat had connected there before hitting his head, likely absorbing some of the blow. Good thing.

She scrambled onto the seat and scooted across to exit through the driver's side. With Bryce's help, he followed Paige toward the house as sirens sounded in the distance.

Once inside, he sank onto the couch. "I'm booking you into a hotel tonight. No arguments."

"I wasn't planning to offer any." Her tone was contrite. "You should just take me back to Atlanta."

His heart twisted at the regret in her dark eyes. "That's not an option."

"As long as I'm here, you're in danger."

"And if you leave, you're dead. I'm going with the first choice." He crossed his arms. "Since you have no transportation and very little money, you're stuck."

The sirens grew to ear-piercing volume, then died midscreech.

She looked down at him, challenge in her eyes. "Why are you so determined to protect me? I'm not your responsibility."

Yeah, he'd had the same thought when he found her. But learning that she was without her memory and essentially defenseless had changed everything. He wasn't any more able to turn his back on her now than he'd been then. And he wasn't going to explain the reasons to anybody.

He pushed himself to his feet and swayed sideways. Her hand shot out to steady him. "All right, you win. But if anything else happens, I'm going home. I'll hitch-hike if I have to."

A knock sounded on the door, and he took a few steps in that direction.

"Sit." The command came from both Bryce and Paige.

He didn't argue. He walked back toward the couch, each step a drumbeat on the inside of his skull, then sank into its softness. Paige stood over him. "You need to have your head checked."

Bryce laughed. "He's been told that before."

"I'm serious." Her tone was stern. "You could have a concussion."

"I've got to get you somewhere safe."

"Hey, you made me go." She gave him a weak smile. "Turnabout's fair play."

Her smile tugged one out of him. "All right."

Bryce swung open the door and invited the officer inside. He couldn't give a description of the attacker beyond a rough estimate of height and build. Tanner didn't even have that much.

Twenty minutes later, the officer was gone. Bryce stood guard outside while Tanner helped Paige pack her meager belongings. Bryce's place a mile away was out of the question. Instead, Paige would be staying at the Hampton Inn in town. She hadn't even put up a fight. Of course, he and Bryce had ganged up on her.

Actually, it had been three against one, since the of-ficer had piped in with the same advice. He'd also promised that a unit would regularly circle the area, looking for anyone suspicious.

Tanner walked her to his truck under Bryce's watchful eye. As he slid into the driver's seat, his friend called to him.

"I'm following you guys, just to make sure you don't have a tail."

"Thanks." He cranked the engine and looked at Paige. "You okay?"

"Okay. Just not thrilled."

"You need to be somewhere safe."

"I know. But I'm afraid of racking up a hotel bill I can't pay."

He backed up from the drive. "You can pay me back when you're able."

"That's what I'm worried about—paying you back. What if I get home and learn I have no savings account and a grand total of $17.31 in my checking account?"

"Then we do an installment plan."

She heaved a sigh. "Moral of the story, I'd better get my memory back before I end up owing you a kidney and my firstborn child."

"Relax. I'm not looking for any kidneys *or* firstborn children." He'd never pictured children of any kind in his future. He wouldn't know what to do with a kid. Colton and Mandy were doing a great job with Liam, but they had examples to follow. Mandy had always had a stable home. Colton had gotten his lessons late, but he'd obviously picked up on the important ones.

Tanner turned left onto the four-lane to head toward town. As he approached Ranger Road, he glanced in his rearview mirror where the Sorento's headlights shone from some distance back. All the way to town, his friend stayed behind them. Finally, the SUV's left-turn signal came on and Bryce pulled over to make a U-turn. They hadn't picked up a tail, but Tanner wasn't about to let down his guard.

Ahead, the light turned red, and he pressed the brake. Paige held up a hand. "Turn here."

"Why?" Even as he asked the question, he flipped the signal and got into the left-turn lane. The green arrow came on, and he accelerated into the turn.

Paige pointed again, right this time. "Pull into the church."

"Murphy First Baptist? Why? No one's here." At almost nine on a Monday night, the interior lights were off and the parking lot was deserted. But spotlights illuminated a tall white steeple.

He drove up the entrance's sharp incline and pulled into a space. The brick structure stood in front of them, wooden beams framing the three entry doors. Above them, stained glass art depicted scenes of Jesus.

"Do you remember something?"

"Not an actual memory. More like a sensation, like when I remembered running through the woods. Except this time, the emotions are all good."

"Maybe a church helped you after you got out of jail."

Paige leaned forward, looking around her. Finally, she sat back and closed her eyes. "This is an important part of my life."

"Church?"

"Church. Ministry. God." She opened her eyes. A streetlight on the corner shone from behind her, putting her in silhouette, but the soft glow of the dashboard lights illuminated her face. "I don't remember how I found Him or when, but I feel Him with me. I have a sense of peace." She paused. "Will you bring me to church here Sunday?"

"That wouldn't be wise. Every time you go out, you risk being seen."

And that got him off the hook. He'd been in Murphy one week, and Colton had already invited him twice. Paige wouldn't have any more success than Colton had had. He didn't do church, had no interest in trying to get to know the God he'd heard about during his childhood—a God who demanded sacrifice and strict adherence to rules but turned His back on a broken-down system full of hurting kids.

Paige sighed. "Maybe we can find a service on TV."

We? There wouldn't be any *we*. Now that Paige remembered she'd gotten religion at some point in her life, he needed to set her straight as soon as possible.

"Feel free to watch whatever you'd like, but I won't be joining you."

"Why not?"

What could he say? That he was boycotting God? He shrugged. "I'm not into church."

Instead of questioning him further, she silently studied him. Beyond her, the glow of the streetlight spilled over him. In spite of its softness, he felt exposed.

"I don't know much about your past except that you grew up in foster care. I'm guessing that could make a kid feel like everyone has deserted him, including God."

For someone who hadn't experienced it, she'd hit the nail on the head. Or maybe she *had* experienced it.

"You know what the shortest verse in the Bible is?" Her tone was soft, serious.

"No, but I'm guessing you do."

"I probably know where it's found, too, but can't call up the reference. *Jesus wept*."

"So?"

"You know why He cried? One of His closest friends had died. Since He was getting ready to raise him from the dead, I don't think He was crying for Himself. I think He was crying for everyone else. You know what that tells me? God sees every tear we shed and grieves with us."

"Hmm." Not an intelligent response, but it was all he could come up with. At the moment, he liked the Paige with no memory better than this one.

He shifted the truck into Reverse. "We'd better get going. I don't like sitting out in the open."

She nodded. "Thanks for stopping. That wasn't a specific memory, but it's a step in the right direction."

Before pulling back out onto Hiawassee Street, he looked right, then left. The pain in his head intensified. He'd probably have a massive headache for the next several days.

But if it meant keeping Paige safe, he'd do it again. Even if he had to put up with her talking about God.

Paige had demanded to know why he was so determined to protect her. The answer was obvious. He'd devoted his life to serving and protecting others. If he was going to dump her in Atlanta with no memory, he might as well put a target on her back.

Or maybe it was because she had no one. And *alone* was a desperate place to be.

Or maybe he was still trying to make up for one fateful night so long ago. A night that upended his world.

Those long, terrifying moments when he should have acted but had done nothing.

FIVE

Tanner stood in the hallway of the Hampton Inn in front of a closed door, a do-not-disturb sign hanging from its knob. He held the strap of an insulated cloth cooler in one hand and a laptop case in the other.

Paige answered his knock. She'd apparently washed her hair. It hung straight and black, glistening in the glow of the lamps. She had the drapes drawn, but every light in the room was on.

"I assume you checked the peephole before opening the door."

"I did." She gave him a crooked smile. "Even with your secret knock."

"I'm afraid my secret knock is the same one the rest of America uses."

He stepped into the room, and she closed the door behind him. Monday night, he'd checked her in under an alias. Tuesday, he'd relayed the events to Colton and Mandy, whose friend was head of Housekeeping. Mandy had assured them Darice could be trusted, so they'd filled her in on everything. Not only was she supplying Paige with towels and toiletries, but she was staying on the lookout for anyone suspicious.

Paige's gaze dipped to the black bag he held. "Is that what I think it is?"

"If you think it's a laptop, the answer is yes. Colton bought a new one sometime back and had this one tucked away in his closet." He removed it from the case and laid it on the table. "Maybe it'll help with the boredom."

Even though it was only Wednesday, being confined in the room had to be driving her crazy. All it took was one look at the tan she sported and the athletic build to know she didn't spend her days lounging in front of the TV. If she ever accompanied him and Bryce on a white-water rafting adventure or a trek through the wilderness, she'd probably be his match. That physical fitness, along with her inner strength, made an enticing combination.

But she might as well be wearing a sign around her neck—*KEEP AWAY* in bold black letters. She had invisible walls a mile thick. Besides, she was taken. Or had been until recently. Whether an engagement ring or a wedding band, she hadn't removed it that long ago. Maybe she'd taken off all her jewelry before leaving home and was still committed. Or maybe she'd ended the relationship. Even then, those decisions weren't always permanent.

Neither scenario boded well for him. He'd already had one woman dump him this year. He wasn't interested in going for round two, even if Paige eventually dropped her guard,

He set the cooler next to the laptop. "I also brought lunch."

He'd stopped at Ingles yesterday and picked up milk, cereal and sandwich fixings, along with some healthy snack options she'd requested. But nothing beat home-cooked meals.

As he unzipped the cooler, she drew in a deep breath. "Mmm, smells like Italian."

"Spaghetti."

She laid out two Styrofoam plates, another Ingles purchase, then added napkins and plastic forks. "How's your head?"

"The pain is starting to lessen."

He'd gone to the emergency room Monday night, after getting her settled. Tuesday he'd taken his share of painkillers. Today he'd had just one so far. Of course, it was only noon.

He pulled a container from the cooler and dished up two generous servings. "And how's *your* head?"

"Empty."

"Everything's there. It's just misfiled."

"That's one way to look at it." She stabbed her fork into the middle of her spaghetti and wound the noodles around the tines. "No new memories. But I slept better last night." She stopped twirling her fork, and her gaze locked with his. "Have I told you how much I appreciate all you're doing for me?"

"Several times."

"I owe you my life."

He waved away her praise. "It's just part—"

"I know, it's just part of your job. Maybe getting me out of the woods and to safety is part of the job. But not everything you've done since. You're a special man, Tanner. I don't remember the other men in my life, but I doubt there are any that top you."

He shrugged, ignoring the awkwardness he always felt with praise, as well as the unexpected warmth spreading through him. "It's nothing, really. You're doing me a favor."

"How's that?"

"You're giving me something to help occupy my time until I start my new job. Otherwise I'd be dying of boredom." The only thing less tolerable than being idle for three weeks in Murphy would have been facing Kevin and Brittney on a daily basis. But it was more than boredom that drove him. Staying busy helped keep the memories at bay.

Not the nightmares, though. He'd had an especially bad one last night, probably triggered by finding the body. Instead of the Nantahala Forest, it was a dingy little bedroom with puke-green shag carpet. Instead of a man, it was a twelve-year-old girl. Instead of finding the decaying body of a stranger, he'd again watched that nasty carpet soak up the lifeblood of his sweet sister.

He shook off the thoughts. "Colton has a pontoon boat, but considering the condition of his kayak after I borrowed it, that's probably out of the question." He forced a smile. The police had recovered it, but the half-dozen holes in the bottom made it pretty worthless. Several times Tanner had tried to pay for it, and Colton had refused. The only chance he'd get to make it right was to show up on Colton's doorstep with a new kayak in tow.

A ringtone sounded on Paige's phone. He picked it up. No one had her number except him and the law enforcement people they'd talked to.

The caller identified himself as Detective Gordon Swisher with Swain County. He had some information and would be there in an hour.

Paige chewed her lower lip. "Are you hanging around?"

"Definitely." With no memory, she needed an advocate.

When there was a knock an hour later, Tanner checked the peephole, then opened the door. The detective stood there, holding a file folder. Tanner invited him in, and after introductions, offered him a chair. Paige took her seat opposite him, and Tanner sat nearby on the foot of the bed.

Swisher opened the folder. "We've identified the body in the woods through prints and tattoos. Thomas Jenkins of Atlanta. Twenty-one years old. Do you know him?"

"The name isn't familiar."

"Here's a picture. Maybe that'll help."

Paige looked down at the sheet he placed in front of her, and her eyes widened. At her sharp intake of air, Tanner tensed. She recognized the man.

Tanner leaned forward. It was a mug shot. The man's hair was as dark as Paige's. A square jaw framed a cocky smile, and his eyes held wildness. Tanner had seen enough people strung out on drugs to recognize the signs. The guy was amped.

"So, you know him." It was a statement rather than a question.

"I think I do. When we found him, I felt…sad. But I can't remember how I know him or who he is."

The detective raised a brow, skepticism written across his face.

Tanner's jaw tightened. "She had a head injury and was left with amnesia."

"That's what the initial report says."

And apparently, he had his doubts.

"Where do you know him from?"

"I don't know."

He narrowed his eyes. "When I showed you the picture, you recognized him."

"Earlier this week, I had a dream. A man got shot in the head. When I woke up, I didn't recognize him." She planted an index finger in the middle of the picture. "This is the man in my dream."

"So you dreamed about the murder."

"I think I was there. The memory surfaced in my dream. At least that part of it did."

"You remember the man being shot. What do you remember leading up to it?"

"Nothing. Just the man being shot."

Swisher shuffled his papers. "Your prints are on both packs, with his over yours on the smaller one."

Paige nodded. "Maybe they both belonged to me and I lent the smaller one to Thomas."

"So you lent him a pack and the two of you set out together to hike the Appalachian Trail. How did you know Jenkins?"

"I. Don't. Know." Exasperation came through in her tone. "I've told you everything I remember."

"Which isn't much."

"Sorry. I'll try to dream in more detail next time."

Tanner stifled a smile at her sarcasm. He didn't need to worry about her needing an advocate. She could hold her own.

Swisher consulted his folder again. "The prints lifted from the canteens have been identified as yours."

"When I was in the woods, I remembered filling canteens. I probably dropped them when I was being chased."

Swisher put the mug shot with the other pages and

closed the folder. "We're searching for Jenkins's next of kin." He pushed himself to his feet. "Obviously, the case is still under investigation. So don't leave the area."

"I have nowhere to go."

Tanner rose and followed Swisher to the door. The detective stepped into the hall, then turned to face him again.

"Total amnesia is pretty rare."

Tanner tightened his grip on the door handle. "But it's not unheard of."

For several moments, Swisher searched Tanner's eyes. Was he looking to see if he was hiding something? Did he think he'd lost his objectivity?

Maybe he had. The man was only asking the tough questions, the same ones *he* should be asking. After all, he'd had his own suspicions, like when she said she didn't know who was holding the knife in the first memory she'd shared.

Sure, he wasn't acting in a law enforcement capacity. He wasn't even actively working. But he was a cop regardless. He needed to think and act like one. All the time. No matter how attractive she was or how she stirred his sense of protectiveness. It was time to find out what she was hiding.

As soon as he closed the door, he turned to Paige. "You need to tell me everything." He was sticking his neck out for her. It was only fair that she come clean with him.

"I have." Her tone held firmness, but there was hurt in her dark eyes.

"Your memory of the knife. You know who was holding it, don't you?"

"I don't—the memory's not that clear. I mean, the details…" Her eyes dipped to the floor.

"Tell me, Paige. Who was it?" Silence stretched. The air was heavy with tension. "What will it take for you to trust me?"

"It has nothing to do with trust. I can't tell you what I don't remember."

He crossed his arms and nailed her with a stern gaze. "I'm guessing one of those Bible verses you know addresses lying."

She glared up at him, lips pressed together. Finally, she threw her hands in the air. "Fine. You want to know who was holding the knife? I was. So go ahead and arrest me."

He put a hand on her shoulder. "I'm not going to arrest you. It's one snippet of memory. We don't know the circumstances."

She sank onto the edge of the bed and put her face in her hands. "I want my memory back. But I'm so afraid of what I'm going to learn. So far I've regained two— my threatening to slit one man's throat and watching another get shot."

When she lifted her head, the anguish in her eyes shot straight to his heart.

"And I can't even say for sure that I wasn't the one holding the gun."

Paige looked away from the laptop screen and tilted her head to one side. Pain shot down the other as tight muscles refused to release.

She'd slept well last night, in spite of the tough conversation she'd had with Tanner. Or maybe it was *because of* the tough conversation. Those memories had weighed heavily on her. Sharing them had been a relief, though everything within her had protested against dropping her barriers.

If she had to let someone into her confidence, Tanner was a good choice. He'd been the voice of reason amid her churning thoughts, insisting that if she'd killed the man in the woods, she wouldn't have had someone shooting at her. Even learning she'd been the one wielding the knife hadn't fazed him. Considering her history, he speculated that she'd had lots of violent moments, and until she could put them into context, she was worrying prematurely.

So she'd slept well. But she'd slept in an awkward position and woken up with a stitch in her neck. An hour of staring at the computer screen had only made it worse.

Now the dull headache she'd ignored for the past week screamed at her. Her granola and milk lay like lead in her stomach. If she didn't take something soon, she was going to be sick.

She reached up to massage her neck and shoulders. It didn't help any more than it had the first dozen times. What she needed was some ibuprofen. Tanner would bring her anything she asked for, but he was tied up at home and wouldn't arrive until after lunch. Why hadn't she gotten that prescription filled when she'd had the chance?

Because taking pills didn't sit right with her, especially ones that could become addictive. It didn't matter that they were prescribed. If she could manage without them, she did.

She returned her attention to the screen, where images of Atlanta lay in neat, unending rows. First, she'd gone to Google Maps and typed in the address the DMV had for her. Satellite view had put her right there, as if she were standing in front of her apartment building. She'd rotated the view, used the 360-degree feature and "walked" around the building.

Now she had random pictures of Atlanta. Hundreds of them. Nothing looked familiar. She might as well have never been there.

She slammed her hand down on the table, frustration seeping through her. Atlanta was her home. How could all memory of it be erased?

Pain rolled through her head, swelling with every beat of her heart. She closed her eyes and massaged the base of her skull. What she wouldn't give for a bottle of painkillers. Nothing narcotic. Not even a whole bottle. Just two little pills.

It didn't help to know she sat within two hundred yards of every kind of painkiller imaginable. A Walgreens pharmacy stood right across the street. She'd appreciate the irony if she wasn't in so much pain.

She rose from the chair and stretched out on the bed. The horizontal position sent blood roaring to her head. She pressed her hands to her skull, willing the pressure to release.

Finally, she sat up, feeling no better than when she'd lain down. Her gaze fell across her jacket, draped over the back of the chair. If she braided her hair and put on the jacket, flipping up the hood, she wouldn't be as conspicuous. She could slip out, buy what she needed and be in the room again in ten minutes flat. She even had the cash.

No, that wasn't an option. Forget the attacker. Tanner would kill her himself. His protective tendencies bordered on obsession. He blamed it on the oath he'd taken. But what he was doing went far beyond career commitment. Maybe someday she'd understand what drove him.

No, she wouldn't. She wasn't going to be there long enough for them to develop that kind of intimacy. As soon as she regained her memory, she'd head home to her life, and he'd return to his. An odd sense of melancholy settled over her.

She picked up the remote and returned to her spot on the bed. Ten minutes later, she turned the TV back off. The light, the movement on the screen and the noise had been a deadly combination.

She pushed herself upright again. The bedside clock said 10:08 a.m. Tanner wouldn't be there for another two or three hours. And she couldn't ask Mandy's friend to leave work and pick her up something.

This was ridiculous. She wasn't someone who depended on others to do what she could do herself. She didn't know how she knew that, but she did. The role of helpless female was too foreign.

After weaving her hair into a sloppy braid, she slid her phone into her jeans pocket and shrugged into the jacket. She'd slip across the street, buy what she needed, then lock herself in her room. Tanner would never know. By the time he arrived, she'd be past the worst of her headache and be a functioning human being.

She flipped the jacket's hood over her head and peeked through the peephole. After swinging the door open, she checked the hallway. It was empty. At the elevator, she pushed the down button. Time was moving at a snail's pace. So was the elevator. How long could it take to go from the first to the third floor?

She glanced over her shoulder, unable to shake the

sensation that someone was going to round the corner and start taking shots at her. She pressed the button three more times in rapid succession.

A ding announced the elevator's arrival, and she dived between the doors before they'd finished opening. When she walked into the lobby, the clerk at the check-in area greeted her. Paige returned the greeting without slowing. She didn't feel nearly as brave as she had in her room.

After waiting for the traffic light to change, she jogged across Pleasant Valley Road and through the Walgreens parking lot. Once inside, the dread began to ease. Other shoppers roamed the aisles, each looking harmless.

She hurried to the pain reliever section and snatched a twenty-four-count bottle of ibuprofen from the shelf. With no one in line at the register, she had her transaction completed in less than two minutes.

Instead of darting outside, she stood at the door for several moments, scanning the parking lot. It was active but not bustling. A pickup truck crossed in front of her, creeping toward the exit onto Andrews Road. A Buick Regal came from the opposite direction and swung into an empty spot. Her hotel was just a few hundred feet away.

When she stepped out the door, the scent of cigarette smoke drifted to her. She glanced left and gasped. A man stood a few feet away, in front of the section of wall separating the entrance from the first double window. His lips curved upward in a smile, but there was nothing friendly about it.

"Hello, Paige." The words sent a chill all the way to her core. She recognized that voice. It was the same one she'd listened to, lying under the hemlock, too scared to breathe.

He swept aside the windbreaker he wore, exposing the pistol holstered at his side, then let the jacket fall into place. "We're taking a little hike." He nodded behind her. "Walk toward Andrews Road and cross."

She looked that direction. Andrews Road ran along the side of Walgreens. The ground on its opposite edge rose upward and disappeared among trees.

She tightened her grip around the bag she held as panic pounded up her spine. He was taking her back into the woods.

She scanned the parking lot. In one space, a mother helped a young child out of a minivan. An elderly gentleman removed a walker from the trunk of the Regal, his wife still inside the car.

"Don't even think about it." Paige tensed at the icy voice beside her. "If you try anything, I'll put a bullet through your gut. And you won't be the only casualty." He tilted his head toward where the young woman had just straightened, the child's hand tucked into hers.

Paige swallowed hard and began walking. Whatever happened, she wasn't going to put anyone else in danger. She should never have left the room. Her attacker had somehow discovered where she was and had probably been watching for her to do something stupid. What had she been thinking?

She hadn't been. Her head had hurt so badly, her sole focus had been on finding relief. The headache was still there, a keen-edged agony that set every nerve ending on fire. But it had taken a backseat to her current predicament. She needed to find a way out. The man wasn't huge. But at six inches taller and fifty pounds heavier, he'd be hard to overpower.

She drew to a stop at the edge of the street and waited for a truck to pass. The driver cast a glance at them but didn't slow.

"Go."

She started at the gruff command. Traffic was clear, but her shoes felt tacked in place. The woods loomed in front of her, thick and ominous, and hopelessness swept through her.

She squared her shoulders. She needed to keep her head. An opportunity for escape would come. When it did, she'd be ready.

He marched her across the street and into the woods. When she turned around a minute later, the road was no longer visible.

Suddenly, he slammed her into a tree so hard, it knocked the breath from her. Before she could react, he pinned her there, with one hand in the center of her chest and the other holding a knife against her throat. Blood roared through her ears, and the bag she held fell to the ground.

She stood stock-still, afraid to breathe. He'd apparently decided not to use the gun. Of course, stabbing her would be quieter than shooting her.

"What do you want?" Her question was a hoarse whisper.

"Tell me what you did with the key and code."

Fog swirled through her mind, the same confusion she'd felt upon awakening in the woods. "What are you talking about?"

"The key and code you got from Torpedo."

"Torpedo?"

"Tommy."

She blinked several times, trying to clear the fog. Tommy? *Thomas Jenkins.*

"He didn't give me anything." If he did, she lost it. Or hid it in the woods, figuring she'd go back to it later. Either way, it wasn't any more accessible to her than it was to him.

"I don't believe you."

The pressure against her chest and throat increased, and her thoughts spun. Who was he? And who was Thomas Jenkins? What relationship did she have with them?

All she knew was that Thomas Jenkins was dead, and she'd witnessed it. Maybe even done it herself. Now there was some kind of key and code involved. If only she could remember.

"You better start talking, fast."

The obvious threat behind his words stopped her thoughts cold. His hand shifted a minute amount. The blade pierced her skin, and moisture trickled down her neck.

Heat built in her chest, her pounding heart carrying liquid fire to every part of her body. In one lightning-fast motion, she twisted and drove her left arm upward and out, knocking away the hand that held the knife. Her other fist connected with the underside of the guy's nose.

Blood spurted in an arc as he swung his head side to side and released a bellow of rage. Without giving him a chance to recover, she peppered his face with a series of punches, then ended with a solid kick between his legs.

He stumbled backward, dropping the knife and reaching under his jacket. By the time he withdrew the pistol, she was on him. She kicked a fraction of a second before he fired, and the shot went wild. The gun tumbled from his grasp, landing in the underbrush several feet to her left.

Instead of trying to retrieve it, he spun and ran toward the road. She glanced at the weapon, then tore off after him. When she broke through the tree line, he was sprinting across Andrews in front of a large box truck. The driver slammed on the brakes and blew the horn. Another vehicle traveled right behind him, and Paige skidded to a stop at the edge of the street.

As she waited for the second truck to pass, her heart pounded and her head throbbed. She swiped a hand across her throat, then drew it away, smeared with blood.

The excitement, the exertion, the adrenaline rush—it was too much. Her stomach heaved, and the breakfast that had refused to digest surged up her throat. When the spasms were nothing more than dry heaves, she straightened and wiped her mouth. The man who'd attacked her had run behind Walgreens and was crossing the next street over, headed toward the woods beside Walmart.

She walked across the street on shaky legs and pulled her phone from her pocket. The first call would be to 911. The police would arrive in minutes. But her attacker would be long gone. This time she could provide a detailed description—height, build, hair color and clothing. And a face that looked like it had encountered a Mack truck.

She stifled a smile. Somewhere along the way, she'd learned how to fight. Quite well.

After finishing the call, she waited inside Walgreens

for the police to arrive. The second call would wait. As long as possible.

She was going to have to talk to Tanner. Even without the obvious cut on her throat, she'd never be able to keep something like this from him. Once she finished with the police report, maybe she'd be ready.

No, she'd never be ready. Because no matter how she sugarcoated what had happened, Tanner would be furious.

And that bothered her way more than it should.

She heaved a sigh. She could go up against the baddest thug in a fight for her life.

But the thought of angering Tanner wrapped her insides in tiny twisted knots.

SIX

Tanner stomped up the final flight of stairs to the third floor. He could have taken the elevator, but that wouldn't have worked out any of the anger that had simmered since the moment he received Paige's call. Actually, the stairs weren't working it out, either.

During the entire twenty-minute drive to town, he'd stewed. If he hadn't been ready to throttle Paige when he left home, he was now.

What had she been thinking? He'd told her not to leave the room or open the door for anyone except him and Mandy's friend Darice. How was he supposed to protect her when she wouldn't even follow simple instructions?

He finished the last flight of stairs and burst into the hall. Yesterday he'd taken her for her follow-up doctor's appointment and hadn't relaxed his vigilance for one second. Today she'd apparently decided she was perfectly safe strolling Murphy alone.

The door swung open moments after he knocked, and he resisted the urge to unload on her right then. No sense calling attention to her unnecessarily. He stepped inside and closed the door behind him.

"I'm sorry." Regret filled her large brown eyes, adding sincerity to the apology. It cooled the fire raging inside but didn't douse it completely. She'd put herself in grave danger for no good reason.

He didn't know the details, just that she'd gone across the street to Walgreens and been accosted on her way back. And she'd insisted she was okay. That was as far as she'd gotten before he shot out the door and made the stress-filled drive to town.

He scanned her from head to toe, heart still pounding out an erratic rhythm. A sense of relief permeated his churning emotions. Her clothes weren't disheveled or torn. No bruises or swelling marred her face. Her hair was even neatly brushed, flowing in front of her left shoulder and down the front of her in an ebony stream.

As she turned to lead him into the room, her hair shifted. He drew his brows together. What had he just seen?

He gripped her shoulder and turned her to face him. A plastic bandage stretched across the left side of her throat. Several inches below that, a dark stain marked the upper edge of her tank.

The fire flared anew. "What happened to your neck?"

"I got cut. Just a nick."

"You said you were fine." He ground out the words.

"I *am* fine. I told you, it's just a nick."

"Someone holds a knife to your throat and cuts you." With each word, his volume grew. "You call that fine?"

"Since all I needed was a Band-Aid, yes, I call that fine." Her tone matched his.

"You're not supposed to leave this room. Do you have a death wish or something? I'm not putting you up in a hotel so you can go traipsing all over Murphy."

She squared her shoulders and stepped closer, but

didn't soften her tone. "I wasn't traipsing all over Murphy. I walked across the street with my jacket on and my hair covered. I didn't think anyone would recognize me."

"A jacket with a hood. You think that's a disguise?"

She heaved a sigh. "I was desperate. I had a horrible headache. I needed some painkillers."

"So you thought you had to venture out and get them yourself." He tipped his head back and tried to rein in his anger. "You know I would have brought you anything you asked for."

"You were busy. I didn't want to bother you."

"Have I ever made you feel like you're a bother? You need to set aside your stubbornness and let yourself depend on someone else for a change."

Her eyes flared. "*Stubbornness? For a change?* Don't act like you know me. You have no idea who I am." She flung her arms wide. "*I* don't even know who I am."

Her voice broke, and she spun away from him. The last of his anger sputtered and died. The strength Paige radiated made it easy to underestimate the toll everything was taking on her.

He put both hands on her shoulders and squeezed. "It's all right. Your memory will come back. Meanwhile, I'm here. So are Bryce and Colton and Mandy."

She turned to face him. Her eyes glistened, but she offered him a small smile. "Thank you."

"Just promise me you won't ever go out alone again."

"I won't. I promise." She cocked her head to one side. "Why are you doing this? Why are you so obsessed with protecting me?"

He opened his mouth to respond, but she held up a hand.

"I don't want to hear it's your job. Your need to protect goes beyond duty. Like it's personal. Something happened, didn't it? Something that left a lasting impression."

Yeah, something happened. But he didn't want to go there. He had no control over what images and memories invaded his dreams, but he wasn't about to revisit those experiences now.

He shrugged. "I'm a guy. We're wired to be protectors. It's why we do things like go to war."

"That's even more lame than 'it's my job.' Come on, you told me I need to trust you. Trust goes two ways, you know."

Yeah, and he still didn't have hers. Last night, she'd given him the details of the incident with the knife. But only because he'd pushed. He'd even used the Bible against her. But he wasn't naive enough to believe he'd had any major breakthrough in getting her to let down her guard.

"Come on. Tell me what's up. I want to understand."

He heaved a sigh. He didn't want to go there, but the words spilled out anyway. "After my mom's boyfriend killed her, he killed my sister."

Her eyes widened, revealing all the pity swimming in their depths. He clenched his teeth. He didn't want pity.

"I'm so sorry. How old was your sister?"

"Twelve."

"And now you've devoted your life to getting guys like him off the street. And protecting the would-be victims."

"Yeah." He pulled out a chair and sank into it. "How's your headache?"

"It's letting up now that I've taken something." She

tilted her head toward the dresser, where a bottle of ibuprofen sat next to the TV. "I'd dropped it in the woods, but picked it up when I showed the police where they could find the weapons."

She eased into the other chair, a smile quivering at the corners of her mouth. "I have to say, though, I fared better than my attacker did. Police are looking for someone with a broken nose, two black eyes and badly swollen lips. He might have gotten a couple of dislocated fingers, too, when I kicked the gun out of his hand."

Tanner's gut tightened. "He had a gun *and* a knife?"

She nodded. "The police have both. He left them in the woods when he ran away."

Tanner shook his head. Unarmed and maybe 120 pounds soaking wet. And she managed to fend off an attack by someone much larger than her. Not just fend off the attack, but effectively launch her own.

"Remind me to never make you mad." He lifted a brow. "So did you learn anything?"

"Besides the wisdom of not going out alone till this is over?"

"I was thinking more along the lines of who this guy might be and what he's after."

"I don't know who he is, but he knows me, called me by name. And he knew Jenkins. He's looking for a code and a key."

"What kind of code and key?"

"No idea. Supposedly Thomas had them and gave them to me."

"Do you think he did?"

She shrugged. "If he did, I can't remember. I obviously don't have them."

He nodded. When he'd found her, her pockets had

been empty, except for that funny little box. He shifted his gaze to the nightstand, where it sat next to the clock. Its drawer hadn't held anything but drug remnants.

Unless… Was it possible the box contained other drawers?

He stood and crossed the room, then picked up the box.

"What are you doing?" Her eyes widened. "You're looking for the key and code."

When he sat on the edge of the bed, she moved to join him, eyes alight with anticipation. He turned the box over. If there was a drawer they hadn't discovered, it was hidden well. As the first one had been.

He pried it open, fighting the resistance of wood against wood. Being out of the elements hadn't done anything for the swelling. It was as tight as it had been a week ago.

Finally, it popped free of the encasement that held it. He tipped the box upward to look into the opening. The back looked solid. When he put his fingers inside and pressed, it didn't move.

He held the drawer next to the box. "Look at this."

She gasped. "There's almost an inch of dead space behind the drawer."

"Enough room to hide a key."

For the next few minutes, he pressed and pried and even brought out his multi-tool. But nothing would budge. He sighed and handed her the box.

She stared down at it. "Maybe we should be using a hammer instead."

"I hate to destroy it." Actually, he hated to destroy anything that still had usable life. He'd always taken exceptional care of everything he had, even as a child. Maybe because he'd had so little.

But this was special. The craftsmanship was amazing. Its maker had joined several types of wood almost seamlessly. Varnish gave the surface a smooth, rich shine.

Paige turned it over and slid her fingers along the bottom. It, too, was constructed of several narrow strips of wood joined together. She gripped the box, pressed both thumbs into the center strip and pushed toward the back. Did the piece shift slightly?

After she struggled with it for several more minutes, he had no doubt. It was intended to move but was stuck as tightly as the drawer had been.

He held out a hand. "Let me try."

After she handed him the box, he worked some more. Eventually, it slid back, uncovering a small piece of wood below the dead space. If he pried it loose, maybe he'd have access to the hidden compartment.

The multi-tool's knife did the trick. But the rectangular piece didn't hide an opening. Instead, two miniature pegs rose from its back, aligning with two holes.

"What is it?"

"A locking mechanism." He laid the piece aside. "These two pegs locked into here and kept this section from moving." Which meant he had to be looking at the bottom of a drawer.

Heart pounding, he pried at the side above where he'd removed the piece. Eventually the drawer pulled open, revealing a folded piece of paper. When Paige reached for it, he held up a hand.

"Let me get some gloves. We probably know who put this in here, but we don't want to destroy prints."

Paige agreed, and he left her alone to retrieve a set

of latex gloves from the Silverado. Back in the room, he unfolded the paper. A key lay inside. Judging from the size, it belonged to a mailbox or padlock.

She pointed at the page, a torn sheet of copy paper with a series of numbers scrawled in the center—4268-645. "What do you think that means?"

"I don't know. It looks like a phone number, but the hyphen's in the wrong place." He laid both items on the nightstand. "We need to turn these over to the police."

"No."

He raised his brows at the determination in her voice.

"The fact that Thomas's killer believes I've got this might be the only thing keeping me alive."

"You can't hold on to this. It's important evidence."

"If I turn these over to the police, I won't have anything to bargain with."

He sighed. "Okay, how about a compromise? I'll make a copy of the paper and have a duplicate key cut. Then we'll turn the originals over to the police."

As she nodded, her cell phone rang from the nightstand. He glanced that way and peeled off the latex gloves. "It's Detective Swisher. You want me to take it?"

"Sure."

As soon as he answered, Swisher's gruff voice came through the phone. "Officer Brody? I take it you're with Paige. We've identified Thomas Jenkins's next of kin."

In the pause that followed, Tanner's gut tightened. Why did he get the feeling that what Swisher had to say would rock Paige's world?

Swisher drew in a breath, the sound audible through the phone. "Thomas Jenkins is Paige's half brother."

Tanner responded with his own long pause. How was

Paige going to react? Would the fact that she couldn't remember him make it easier or more difficult?

"I'll let her know."

When he disconnected the call, Paige was watching him, curiosity in her eyes. "I get the impression that was bad news."

He nodded. "Police have figured out the connection between you and Jenkins. He's your half brother."

Her gaze broke from his face and fluttered to her hands. "I don't know what to say. I should feel grief, but I don't. Instead, there's a cold hole where my heart should be." Her eyes again sought his. "Does that make me a horrible person?"

"Not at all. How can you grieve someone you can't remember?" He put an arm around her. "When we found the body, you were sad. You knew he was someone you cared about. That makes you human. Learning he was your brother is just an abstract fact without your memory. Abstract facts don't trigger emotion."

"Thank you." She gave him a shaky smile, then tilted her head toward the items they'd retrieved. "I think it's time to go home."

His chest clenched. "What?"

"I have to return to Atlanta. It's the only way I'm going to unlock my past."

"You need to give it time."

"I have. And I'm no closer to getting my memory back now than I was a week ago." She stood and spun to face him. "I need to find out why my brother was killed, what this key and code are, and why someone wants them so badly. I won't be safe until I do, no matter where I am."

"You'll get your memory back. Don't be in a hurry."

"Can't you see?" She flung one arm to the side, palm raised. "This isn't working. Nothing's familiar here." She sighed. "When I was kneeling at the creek, I remembered filling the canteens. It was a small memory, but it was a start. I need to go where things are familiar, even if just for the day."

His jaw tightened. "In case you've forgotten, you have a killer after you."

"And he found me right here in Murphy."

He clenched his teeth. As angry as he'd been with Paige for putting herself in danger, there was one nagging suspicion he couldn't ignore.

He'd led the killer to her.

He'd been so careful. Every time he'd come to visit, he'd parked some distance away and walked, constantly glancing around, making sure no one was watching.

But someone had been. And Paige's leaving the hotel had given him just the opportunity he'd been waiting for.

She heaved a sigh. "I can't do this anymore. I have to find my past."

Her eyes locked with his, the determination there shutting down any argument he might pose.

"I'm going back to Atlanta, even if I have to walk."

Paige stared through the windshield of Tanner's truck as he sped under the sign announcing the US 41 ramp ahead. According to the GPS, this was their exit off I-75. Traffic was heavy, but it was moving at a good clip. The fact that it was Saturday helped. In another ten minutes, they'd be at their destination.

As they'd approached the city, the skyscrapers rising into the gray sky had looked familiar, probably from the pictures she'd pored over rather than any long-term memory. Today she'd be all over Atlanta. If that didn't trigger some memories, nothing would.

Tanner signaled to take the ramp, and she flipped down the visor. The mirror reflected large sunglasses under spiky blond hair. Cherry-red lipstick accented her mouth.

The only way Tanner would agree to the trip was if she donned a disguise. And he'd made it clear that her jacket didn't qualify. The wig was left over from a costume party Mandy had attended several years earlier. The sunglasses were hers, too.

At least he hadn't borrowed the lipstick. He'd picked that up new at Walgreens. She'd probably never use it again. Whatever her usual look was, bright red lips and spiky blond hair probably wasn't it.

After several turns, Tanner pulled into the parking lot of her apartment complex. People milled around in groups of two or three, talking over beer and cigarettes. Her attacker wasn't among them. If he was hiding somewhere, he wasn't likely to shoot her in front of so many witnesses.

"Do you remember anything?"

She shook her head, then shifted her gaze toward the building. Rusted metal staircases zigzagged up walls of cracked stucco. Duct tape made a diagonal path down two of the windows, and several sections of aluminum soffit had fallen, leaving ends of rafters exposed.

"Apparently I don't live like you do." She almost laughed at the absurdity of her words. That was the understatement of the year.

He might not be thinking it, but her brain had instantly leaped to the obvious conclusion. If this was all she could afford, how was she ever going to satisfy her debt?

"I'll find a way to pay you back, even if I have to make monthly payments."

"I'm not worried about it. If you are, we'll discuss it once you get your life back." He rested a forearm on the top of the steering wheel. "Relax and see if anything comes back to you."

She pulled her lower lip between her teeth, her gaze following the staircase upward and settling on her apartment. What did it look like inside? She closed her eyes and let her head fall back against the seat.

The door stood before her, crystal clear, with its smudges and chips and peeling paint. She imagined reaching for the knob, turning it, swinging the door inward inch by inch, stepping over the threshold into...

Nothing.

Not even empty rooms with bare, undecorated walls. Not even an image borrowed from a long-ago movie.

She heaved a sigh and opened her eyes. "I'm sorry."

"It'll come." He stretched across the console to squeeze her shoulder.

His touch grounded her, the only thing stable in a world that had suddenly switched poles. What would it be like to have the encouragement and support of a man like Tanner on a permanent basis? Forever.

She shook off the thought. She'd never know. Men like Tanner were few and far between. Though she'd thanked God for allowing their paths to cross, she wasn't holding on to hope that their relationship would be anything but temporary. When men like Tanner considered *forever*, they looked for women like Mandy—stable, secure, upstanding citizens—not former gang members who'd spent 20 percent of their lives behind bars.

Tanner dropped his hand from her shoulder. "What do we do now?"

"I can't get into my apartment, because I don't have the key." She'd tucked the one Tanner had had cut into her pocket, but it wasn't going to open any apartments.

"Maybe you don't need one."

She lifted a brow. "Are you suggesting I break in?"

"Maybe you have a roommate. Let's see if someone's home."

She gave him a sharp nod. He'd been eyeing those hanging around and had apparently come to the same conclusion she had.

As she made her way toward the stairs, the two men standing closest followed her with their eyes. Tanner's presence brought a measure of comfort.

She climbed the rickety stairs. Something stirred, more a sense of déjà vu than a bona fide memory. She'd done this before, climbed these exact steps, held on to this rusted metal railing.

When she got to the top, voices sounded from the other side of the door. And music. The TV was on. Someone was there. Or maybe she'd left it on herself to give the appearance that someone was home.

She rapped on the door. A half minute later, it opened two inches. A chain prevented it from opening any farther. From what she could see, the woman looked to be in her early to midtwenties, Hispanic and about Paige's height.

And she had kind eyes. They sparkled with enthusiasm and life. She was just the kind of roommate Paige had hoped she'd have.

Except there was no sign of recognition in those dark eyes.

Paige frowned. She'd only been gone a week. At least that was how long she'd been out of touch. Had they given her apartment away already?

The disguise. Of course.

She smiled but resisted the urge to tear off the wig. "It's me, Paige."

The woman tipped her head to one side, vertical creases above her nose. "Do I know you?"

"Uh…maybe not." She looked to Tanner for help.

"I think we have the wrong apartment. Sorry to bother you."

"No bother. I hope you find who you're looking for."

The door closed with a soft thud, and the dead bolt clicked over. Paige turned with a sigh. Another dead end. As she started down the stairs, tension crept across her shoulders. The men who'd watched her exit the truck were standing below.

When she and Tanner reached the bottom, one stepped forward, brows raised. "Paige?"

Panic spiraled through her. How did he recognize her with the wig and sunglasses?

"Great hair. I wouldn't have known it was you if you hadn't said your name."

That was it. She'd introduced herself to the lady in the apartment. She needed to be more careful. This was supposed to be a covert search mission. But he seemed genuinely happy to see her. She was inclined to put him on the "friend" instead of "foe" side.

"What are *you* doing back?"

Back? That meant she'd lived here but left. The DMV was behind. Which was likely *her* fault.

She shrugged. "I decided to visit the old neighborhood." Hopefully that made sense and she hadn't just moved around the corner. "Do you know about how long I've been gone? I was trying to remember when I moved so I could tell my friend."

He tipped up the amber-colored bottle and took a swig. "You were still here for a while after Christmas. So three months, maybe." He turned to the other guy. "Right?"

He shrugged. "Something like that."

So he knew her, too. She wasn't sure about him. He wasn't putting out the same friendly vibes as the guy who'd complimented her on her hair. Actually, she wasn't sure what kind of vibes she was getting, but they weren't good. She shook off her apprehension. She knew what the killer looked like. This wasn't him.

They walked away from the pair and when Tanner opened the passenger door, she climbed into the truck.

Tanner slid into the driver's seat and closed the door. "Do you remember those guys we were just talking to?"

"No. I don't remember my apartment, either. But I do remember climbing the stairs to get to it." Sort of.

"You want to drive around the area and see if anything looks familiar?"

She nodded. That was as good a plan as any, since going home wasn't an option.

As Tanner pulled from the parking lot, she glanced in the side mirror. The man who'd spoken with her was still hanging out. The other one was gone.

Someone in that apartment complex could probably help her piece together her past. But without knowing who was after her and what connections he had, she couldn't risk it. If only she knew who she could trust.

Tanner made a turn, then drove up and down the streets east of the apartment complex. Many of the buildings had bars on the windows, and graffiti decorated several walls. Men stood on sidewalks, watching them as they passed, and she double-checked the door locks.

The neighborhood south of there wasn't any better. She'd apparently lived at the edge of one of the scariest areas in Atlanta. That wasn't surprising. After five years in prison, she'd have been starting from scratch. No job, no money. And likely no friends, since she'd relocated from Florida.

"Anything look familiar?"

She frowned. "I don't remember this exact location, but the scene is familiar. Bars on the windows, graffiti everywhere, what look to be gang members standing on the corners. It's dark and depressing, but somehow feels like home. I think I grew up surrounded by this."

"But you were apparently working your way out of it. Now, if we could figure out where you went."

Tanner made several more turns. He seemed to be working in a one- or two-mile radius from where they started. They were now west of her old apartment complex. For having traveled so little distance, the difference was amazing.

Vacant houses with boarded windows and overgrown lawns dotted both sides of the street. But interspersed among them were other homes, old and small, but well kept. A door opened and an elderly woman stepped out, purse clutched in one hand. After inserting a key into the lock, she turned and walked toward the dented compact sitting in the drive.

Tanner drove past, and Paige turned in her seat,

drawn to the old woman. There was something familiar about her, the way she walked or the way she was dressed. Or the purse.

That was it. The way she was toddling along, clutching the purse.

Tanner hit the brakes. "Do you remember something?"

"I'm not sure." Did the woman remind her of her grandmother?

As she turned back around, Tanner pulled to the side of the road. She closed her eyes and tried to grasp the memory that danced at the edge of her mind, shrouded in mist. A little old lady walking down a sidewalk, clutching a purse. Something was significant about the purse.

The mist parted and the scene played out. Pounding footsteps. The lady turning and stumbling sideways as the purse was ripped from her grasp. Paige's own breath coming in short pants as she tore down the sidewalk while behind her, a shaky voice uttered cries of protest.

Her eyes snapped open. What? She snatched purses from little old ladies? *Dear God, am I really that horrible of a person?*

No, not *am. Was.* Whoever she used to be, she wasn't that person anymore. Bits and pieces of another Bible verse floated through her mind. Something about being a new creation, the old being gone, everything becoming new.

"What did you remember?"

She released a slow breath. She didn't need to look at Tanner to know that he was watching her. And to know she wasn't going to be able to evade his question. She closed her eyes and tipped her head back. She'd just stolen that lady's purse.

But she hadn't enjoyed it. The experience had actually been…traumatic. She was young. Preteen. And it was the first time she'd ever stolen anything.

She opened her eyes and looked at Tanner. "One brief memory from my childhood. Nothing I can put into context, to borrow your words." She forced a smile, but she'd made it clear with her tone. The conversation was over.

Tanner nodded, then shifted his foot from the brake to the gas. While he drove, she stared out the window, elbow on the armrest, jaw resting against her fist. Soon they reached an area that was mostly commercial or industrial. Ahead, a sign announced Self-Storage, First Month Free.

As Tanner moved past, she dropped her fist to her lap and sat up straight. "Wait. I know that place."

Tanner glanced in his rearview mirror and turned on his left signal. "What place?"

"The storage facility."

A minute later he pulled onto the property and stopped in front of the office. To their right were two wrought iron gates, one leading in and one leading out of the storage area. A small metal box stood on a post in front, no doubt a keypad to open the gate and allow customers access. Why was this place important? Had she rented a unit?

Tanner killed the engine. "Do you want to go inside and talk to someone?"

"I don't know." The clerk probably wouldn't tell her anything without identification. Even if she had something stored here and knew the unit number, she wouldn't be able to get in without a key.

She gasped at the same time Tanner spoke. "The code and key. You have a storage unit here."

He cranked the truck and backed from the space. By the time he got to the keypad, she'd pulled the paper and key from her back pocket.

"Punch in 4268."

Nothing happened.

"Try the whole thing—4268-645."

A few seconds later, a *whir* sounded and the gate began to swing away from them.

Tanner drove through, then stopped. "I'm guessing your unit is number 645. It's part of the code so they can track who goes in and out."

He drove past two rows of units, checking the signs posted at their ends. "Here, 601 through 680."

As he crept closer, she clutched the key in a palm that had grown suddenly moist.

This was it. Another piece of the puzzle of her life.

And something told her it was going to be huge.

SEVEN

Tanner stood next to Paige as she inserted the key into the padlock and turned it. It clicked open.

As he rolled the door up on its track, sunlight flooded the ten-by-twelve space. His heart sank until it wobbled to a stop between his knees.

The left two-thirds of the unit were filled, front to back. He counted eight large-screen TVs. Other electronic devices were stacked around them—DVD players, gaming consoles, speakers, monitors. Jewelry boxes lay on top of some of the stacks. Several backpacks sat in front, names like Canon and Nikon giving away what was inside. Other flatter cases probably contained laptops and iPads.

Tanner swallowed the bile working its way up his throat. What he was looking at meant one thing. And Paige was involved. He'd have to call the police.

When he turned to say so, his chest clenched.

She'd taken off the sunglasses and slid them over the wig. She now stood with her arms crossed over her stomach, eyes wide and face pale. "This can't be mine. I wouldn't be dealing in stolen property."

There wasn't any conviction in her tone. Instead, it

held a plea, as if she was begging a higher power to let what she said be true.

But God wasn't going to help her out of this one. As much as Tanner wanted to, he couldn't deny the facts. She remembered the unit. It had to be hers.

But Thomas had the key and code. Her attacker even said so. And Thomas was her brother. Maybe she knew the location of his storage unit without knowing what was inside.

When he pulled his phone from his pocket, her face paled even more. He hesitated. "We've got to call the police. They'll get to the bottom of this. You got the key and code from Thomas, so this stuff is probably his." That was what he'd believe until evidence proved him wrong.

He punched in the three numbers. "Don't touch anything. You don't want to leave prints."

She nodded but didn't speak. Fear filled her eyes, and worry lined her face. His heart twisted, but instead of moving to her side, he stepped through the open door. Cell service would be better outside the metal structure.

When he finished the call and walked back into the unit, Paige stood near the back, staring into an open box.

He rushed toward her. "I told you not to touch anything."

When she looked at him, her face had lost even more color. "This is mine."

He looked into the box. A high school yearbook lay on top. "Maybe it's your brother's."

"No." She pointed at the script on the cover. "If I'm twenty-eight, this would be the year I graduated."

"Maybe it belongs to a friend of his." Okay, he was

grasping at straws. The problem was, he really didn't want it to be true. He liked and respected Paige. She'd overcome incredible odds. It wasn't just the recent events in her life that had impressed him. She'd apparently had a rough upbringing. She'd joined a gang and done hard time, but still walked away from a life of crime.

At least that was what he'd believed until two minutes ago. Now he wasn't sure.

"Look at the box."

He did as she said. An Amazon logo marked the side. She pressed down the top flaps to reveal the shipping label. It was addressed to Paige Tatem, at the apartment where they'd just stopped. Two other boxes sat with this one, these without labels.

Sirens sounded in the distance. Maybe they were responding to another call. Or maybe they were coming here. To take Paige away.

He glanced around them. Other than the electronics and the three boxes, the unit also held a duffel bag. It was lying near the back, partially on its side, as if someone had thrown it into the unit. The zipper was four inches shy of closing completely, leaving the top to gape open.

Tanner approached and clicked the flashlight app on his phone. Without touching the bag, he squatted to angle the beam through the gap. A rubber band stretched beside the face of Ulysses S. Grant.

The sirens grew to ear-piercing volume, then fell silent. The patrol cars were apparently right out front.

He straightened and faced Paige.

"What's in there?" Her voice sounded hollow in the sudden silence.

"Money. I don't know what denominations, but there's a fifty on top." He held out a hand. "Let's go meet the police." He didn't think Paige would run, but he wouldn't take that chance.

He reached for the padlock she'd laid on one of the DVD players when they'd entered. Movement in his peripheral vision snapped his attention to the doorway. The police couldn't have gotten into the compound that quickly.

"Hands up."

He'd been right. It wasn't the police. A man stood there, dressed the same as several others they'd seen that morning in a bandanna, jeans and a sleeveless white undershirt. Except this one was holding a pistol. With a misshapen and discolored nose, bruised cheeks and jaw, and one eye swollen shut, he'd obviously been at the bad end of some angry fists. Probably Paige's.

"You're in the wrong place at the wrong time." He tilted his head toward Tanner, then shifted his gaze to Paige. "But I'm going to enjoy killing *you*."

Tanner's mind spun. He was armed, but he'd never have the opportunity to draw. "If you fire that gun, cops are going to be all over you before you get two doors down. Those sirens you heard are right out front." He took a step back. "I know what you're here for." He took another step. "There's a duffel full of money." When he reached it, he lowered himself into a squat, one arm stretched behind him, the other still raised. "Take it and go." He straightened and tossed the bag.

The man caught it with one arm. "On the floor, face-down."

He dropped to his hands and knees and lowered himself to the concrete. Paige did the same. Was the man still planning to shoot them?

Tanner squeezed his eyes shut and waited. Footsteps sounded, retreating, pounding the asphalt outside.

As he rose, a sharp command rang out nearby.

"Freeze!"

More footsteps. Multiple sets this time. Tanner darted out the door in time to see the man who'd held them up drop the bag and hurl himself over the back fence. One cop hit the fence two seconds later while a second recovered the bag. Storage facility personnel had apparently let them in.

Tanner waited at the unit with Paige while another siren drew close and stopped. Maybe the cop had been successful in his pursuit and their attacker was about to be transported to the jail.

Soon an officer approached them. "Tell me what's going on."

Tanner stepped forward. "I think we've discovered a stash of stolen property. But I'd better start at the beginning." He held out a hand. "Tanner Brody, formerly Louisville PD. Now Murphy, North Carolina, PD. At least I will be in another two weeks."

As he relayed everything he knew about Paige, another law enforcement officer entered and began dusting for prints. Finally, the first officer looked up from his pad, where he'd been furiously taking notes. "So, I take it you don't remember any of this, other than that your brother apparently rented a storage unit here?"

"That's right."

"We're working on lifting prints, but in the meantime, let's go to the office and see what we can find out about the rental of this unit."

As Tanner walked with Paige behind the officer, he tried to ignore the dread pressing down on him. The unit had to belong to Jenkins. He'd passed the code and key to Paige and told the killer as much, probably to save his hide.

It hadn't worked. And he'd put his sister's life in danger. Tanner had never met the man, but he already didn't like him.

The officer walked into the office and approached the desk. "I need to get some information on the rental of one of your storage units." He consulted his notes. "Unit 645."

The assistant keyed something into her computer, then leaned toward the monitor. "That unit is rented to Paige Tatem."

Paige gasped beside him, and he resisted the urge to wrap a protective arm around her.

The officer jotted the information on his pad. "Do you know Paige Tatem?"

"No, I don't." Her eyes shifted to Paige. "I assume this is her. I just started two weeks ago, so I haven't met a lot of our customers."

"When someone rents a unit, is there some kind of contract they have to sign?"

"A rental agreement." She walked to one of three file cabinets that lined the wall behind her, then pulled a folder from the drawer. When she returned, she laid two stapled sheets on the counter between them.

The officer flipped to the second page. In the center, what appeared to be Paige's signature occupied the line, next to a date of January 21. Right around the time when she moved from the apartment, according to the man they'd met this morning.

The door behind them opened and the other law enforcement person walked in. "Several serial numbers came back hot."

The officer they'd been speaking with turned to Paige. "Paige Tatem, you're under arrest for theft by receiving stolen property."

Tanner held up a hand. "Wait." He turned to the clerk. "Do you have any information on who has been making the rental payments?"

"If the payment was mailed, we'd just key the date and check number into the computer. But if someone walked in and paid by check or cash, we'd give them a handwritten receipt."

She reached for a spiral-bound book that stood next to several loose-leaf binders. After flipping it open to the current week, she worked her way backward. "March 21. The payment was made by cash. The receipt is made out to Paige Tatem." She flipped several more pages. "February 20. Same thing—cash, Paige Tatem. And…January 21, which would be the initial payment. This one was by check. Number 307, Paige Tatem."

Why would she make the first payment by check and the other two by cash? Maybe she *didn't* make the cash payments. "If someone brought cash in for someone else, who would you make the receipt out to?"

"Probably whoever they asked us to. Then we'd note the unit number on the receipt."

Tanner nodded. Anyone who would turn a killer on his sister wouldn't think twice about setting her up to take the fall for being in possession of stolen merchandise.

Tanner glanced at the officer, who was now scowling. He probably thought he was trying to get Paige off.

Maybe he was. But only if she was innocent. His gut told him she was. Or maybe that wasn't his gut talking. Maybe what he was listening to was a few inches higher. His heart.

He could no longer deny it. Somewhere between finding her unconscious in the woods and walking through the door of that storage unit, she'd become more to him than a victim in need of protection. And although he'd previously thought of a dozen reasons to keep his distance, at the moment, every one of them eluded him.

Regardless of whatever feelings he'd developed for her, with no memory she had no defense. She needed someone in her corner, someone to push for the truth rather than grasp the easy solutions.

"What if someone let another person take over their unit?"

"If that happens, they're supposed to make the change in here with us. But if they don't, everything ends up staying in the name of the original customer."

"And you make the receipts out however you're instructed."

"Probably."

Tanner turned to the officer. "Please hold off arresting her until the prints come back. Let me take her to Murphy. I'll be responsible for her."

The officer leaned against the counter, one arm resting on its laminate surface, the other hand on his hip. "You're asking me to not only let her leave the city and county but also the state."

"Temporarily. Only until we know for sure she's guilty."

He unclipped the handcuffs from his belt. "The storage unit is in her name. It's her signature on the contract. Her personal items are in the unit." He stepped behind Paige to clip a cuff around one of her wrists. "You have the right to remain silent…"

As Tanner listened to the officer read Paige her rights, the emotion on her face sucker punched him right in the gut. She was lost and alone. And she was afraid. No, terrified.

The officer led her outside, and Tanner followed. "I'll do everything I can to get to the bottom of this."

At the car, Paige turned. When her eyes met his, she raised her chin. "I'll be okay. This isn't my first arrest. It's not even my first time going to jail for someone else's crime."

What? She'd apparently remembered something else.

The officer helped her into the cruiser and closed the door. Her shoulders were back, her chin up. She was putting forth a brave front.

But it was an act.

Granted, she'd ridden in the back of a patrol car before. But this trip was different. This time she had almost no experiences to draw on. Few memories of the rough childhood that had forged her into a strong, tough adult. Little recollection of the things that had guaranteed her survival while running with gangs. Not even the knowledge to formulate her defense.

Every anchor that had secured her had been stripped away and left behind somewhere along the Appalachian Trail.

Paige carried her tray through the chow hall, avoiding the other inmates. The scent drifting upward wasn't entirely disgusting, but it wasn't pleasant, either. Definitely not Tanner's cooking.

She took her place at an empty table with her chin held high, feigning a confidence she didn't feel. In here, showing weakness could be fatal. Even without her memory, she knew that much.

The problem was she didn't feel strong.

Tanner had done everything he could to defend her. She didn't even know if she deserved it. He seemed to believe in her more than she believed in herself.

Every new discovery cast more doubt on her character. From the very first memory with the knife, it had only gotten worse.

The storage unit was hers. Her stuff was in there. Maybe her brother was involved, since he had possession of the key and code. But she was apparently in cahoots with him.

And she'd been there when he was killed. The image of that fatal shot was crystal clear.

A hard shove from behind jolted her out of her reverie. She stood and twisted to find three women staring her down, arms crossed and eyes narrowed. She'd been so lost in her thoughts she'd let them sneak up on her. Now she was pinned against the table.

Without taking her eyes from the largest of the three, she pushed her chair aside with her foot. "You got a problem?"

"Yeah, we do." The woman's eyes dipped to Paige's sleeve.

Paige didn't have to follow her gaze to know what she'd seen. Her shirtsleeve left the bottom inch of her tattoo exposed. Two inches if she reached for something.

She'd been concerned about it from the moment of intake. The tattoo made her the enemy of all rival gangs.

The fact that she was having it removed made her the enemy of her own.

The larger woman pressed closer and the ones on either side took her lead, forming a semicircle of hard flesh that blocked any way of escape.

"You trying to disown us?" Her lips drew back in a sneer.

Several others gathered around. But they weren't there to help her. They were there for the entertainment.

A chant started up, softly at first, then growing in volume. "Fight, fight, fight…"

Paige tightened her hands into fists and positioned them in front of her. She wouldn't throw the first punch, but if she was going down, someone was going with her.

A punch came from the right, a left hook that caught her off guard. She twisted to the side at the moment of contact. It wasn't a direct hit, but was hard enough to make her see stars. She shoved the woman backward, then leaped toward her to counter with several rapid punches of her own.

A fist slammed into her cheek, and pain exploded through her face. But she managed to block several more strikes while continuing her own assault.

Then something glinted in her peripheral vision, metal and plastic. She raised an arm to block the blow but was too late. The chair crashed down on her, the side of a metal leg gashing her forehead. Blood ran into her eyes and down her face.

She continued to swing, her punches going wild. Another blow met her left temple. Her neck snapped and blackness encroached.

"Break it up." A voice boomed over the chaos.

But the beating continued. Her ears rang and the

darkness grew, creeping inward. She dropped to her knees, and a punch landed in her gut. Or maybe it was a kick. The ringing in her ears grew louder and the other sounds faded.

"I said 'break it up.'" The call came again, sounding far away, yet closer.

She toppled sideways and curled into a ball. One more kick landed against her left kidney.

Everything faded and she drifted on a sea of cotton. The blows had stopped, or she was somehow floating above them, her mind no longer connected to her body.

There was movement, something flat under her, soft yet firm. The rumble of wheels against vinyl tile surrounded her.

Then bright lights, visible through her closed eyelids. The movement stopped, and a voice called to her, soft and feminine. She couldn't make sense of the words.

But she was safe. Iris had come to her rescue, that six-foot-two-inch giant of a woman, tough as nails, but gentle as a lamb. She'd stepped in and defended her when members of a rival gang had caught her alone and decided to teach her a lesson.

No, Iris was at Lowell, in Florida. This wasn't Lowell. It was…somewhere else.

"Paige, can you hear me?"

There was that voice again. She tried to open her eyes, but her eyelids were so heavy. Or maybe they were swollen shut. Sealed and caked with dried blood. Maybe they would never open again.

"Paige, I need you to wake up and look at me."

She forced one eye open, then shut it again. The lights were too bright. Her head hurt, too. So did her stomach and back and every other part of her body. Where could she go to escape the pain?

She opened her eyes and tried to sit up. Gentle hands stopped her.

"Whoa, take it easy. You've been in a nasty fight. You need to let me assess your injuries."

"Iris?" She rolled her head to one side, then the other. No one was there except the doctor lady. Or nurse.

"Do you know where you are?"

"Lowell Correctional—" No, she'd already figured that out. She was somewhere else. There was a storage unit. Stolen property. She couldn't remember the details. "Atlanta." The name of the facility escaped her.

"What day is it?"

"Sunday." She'd planned to go to chapel service this afternoon. This was going to interfere with those plans. Iris would be disappointed.

No, Iris wasn't there. And suddenly she missed her desperately.

The first two years at Lowell, Paige had hated her. She'd hated the way Iris never retaliated when others gave her a hard time. She'd hated the way she was continually smiling. And she'd hated the Christian platitudes that always spewed from her mouth.

When Iris saved her life, risking her own in the process, Paige had finally been ready to listen. The next three years, Iris had nurtured her from a brand-new Christian who had so many bad habits she thought she'd never overcome them all, into someone who devoted her life to helping other people out of the bondage she'd lived in for so long.

She sat up suddenly. "I remember."

Maybe not everything, but she remembered large

chunks. Iris. Her time at Lowell. Her decision to leave Orlando and start over in Atlanta. Her work with the inner-city mission.

"I remember." As badly as her face hurt, she couldn't stop the smile climbing her throbbing cheeks. Soon laughter bubbled inside, rumbled up her throat and over-flowed in unrestrained glee. "Thank You, Jesus!"

"Honey, I think you'd better lie back down."

Paige complied, wincing as screaming muscles pro-tested against the change in position. But the laughter continued.

Her memory hadn't fully returned. She still didn't re-member Thomas or why she was on the trail with him. And she had no idea why there was a storage unit with her name on it, full of stolen merchandise.

But this was a start. The rest would come. In the meantime, she had her relationship with the Lord.

No matter what happened, she wasn't alone.

She'd never be alone again.

EIGHT

Tanner shifted position for the fortieth time and tried to return to the legal thriller he'd downloaded on his phone. He'd been sitting in the lobby of the Atlanta City Detention Center since four. Now it was almost six.

The last two days, he'd made enough calls to the storage facility that he could now hear fatigue in the receptionist's voice. He'd gotten the name and contact information of the prior administrative person. Then he'd called back to ask if they tracked the gate codes that were entered. They did, which helped narrow down how much surveillance video they'd have to look at. When he asked if he could view the footage, the woman told him Atlanta PD had already requested it.

He'd also been in touch with the detective assigned to the case and talked him into trying to get the prints expedited. Shortly after three, he'd gotten the news he'd been waiting for. And now Paige was free. Or she would be once the jail finished the last of the red tape.

Finally, the door into the waiting area swung open and a woman stepped through. After a quick glance, he averted his gaze. She looked rough, with one eye swollen shut, her lower lip split and puffy, and her skin a patch-work of yellow, blue and purple.

Wait. Those jeans and tank.

He shot to his feet. A lump formed in his throat, and her name came out as a strangled yelp. When he wrapped her in his arms, she stiffened and groaned.

He released her and stepped back. "What happened?"

"Some of the inmates decided to use me as a punching bag."

"When?"

"Yesterday. Lunchtime. They didn't like my tattoo. Actually, the tattoo was okay. They didn't like the fact that I was having it removed. A corrections officer broke it up."

As he led her to the door, his stomach churned. She'd needed him, and he hadn't been there. He'd failed. Again.

The door swung shut behind them, and she continued, "I spent the rest of yesterday and most of today in the infirmary. Then they came and got me and said I was being released."

"I wish I could have made it happen sooner." Like before lunchtime yesterday.

"Since there hasn't been time for a bond hearing, I'm assuming the charges have been dropped."

"It took some finagling, but it's done."

"Thank the Lord."

Thank the Lord? He'd worked his tail off the past two days. The Lord didn't have a whole lot to do with it.

Paige tossed a bag into the truck and climbed in. "Mandy's wig and sunglasses."

"I'll get them back to her."

She cast him a sideways glance under one puffy eye-lid. "Okay, tell me how you did it. The evidence against me was pretty convincing."

"The first thing I did was push to get the prints expedited. While I was waiting on those, I called the storage place. Before Saturday, the last time someone used the code was two and a half weeks ago. The video surveillance shows Tommy with the duffel. Before that, they caught him on camera several times moving electronics in and out. The last footage of you was in mid-February, hauling out boxes."

He drove onto I-20 and headed for 75. "I also tracked down the former employee. After seeing your brother's mug shot, she confirmed he was the one who made the February and March payments. He told her you wanted your name on the receipts."

She frowned. "He was throwing me under the bus."

"I think that was his normal MO."

He turned on his signal to take the 75 North ramp. "I assume it's okay if we go to Murphy now."

"Yeah. I've seen enough of Atlanta to last me a few days." She laid her head back against the seat. "What about the prints?"

"Yours were on the lock and the warehouse door. The three boxes, too."

"And the guy who held us up?"

"Joseph Blanton, street name Ace. They arrested him, but he's not talking. The duffel he took had heroin in it, too. Police think it's connected with a drug deal that went bad at the same time Thomas put it in the unit. Apparently several people got shot, and someone made off with the money and the drugs."

"That *someone* was probably my brother. What about all the TVs and stuff?"

"Not a single print of yours. Plenty of Thomas's, plus a bunch of others that haven't been identified yet."

She crossed her arms without lifting her head. "I must have been insane to share a storage unit with my brother."

"We usually have a soft spot for family members. It can get in the way of smart decisions."

"Apparently so." She rested her head against the side window, arms still crossed. They were coming up on the 575 exit that would take them toward Murphy.

But Paige wasn't going to stay conscious that long. Every time he glanced at her, her eyes had grown a little heavier. By the time he left 75, they were closed. She remained asleep for the next hour and a half.

He stopped at a traffic light, and her eyes fluttered open. "I fell asleep."

"I noticed."

She started to rub her face, then winced. "Where are we?"

"On 64, a few miles from downtown." He stepped on the gas. "What do you think of restaurant fare?"

"Awesome. Especially after two days of prison food."

"Good." He handed her his cell phone. "How about searching restaurants that offer takeout? Maybe we should go back to the hotel."

"Let's eat inside. We need to celebrate. The creep who killed my brother and has been after me is behind bars."

His stomach tightened. "What if there's more than one?"

"There isn't. I recognized the voice. The guy at the storage unit, the one at Walgreens and the one in the woods—all the same guy."

He frowned. He still wasn't ready to let down his guard. Maybe he was just having a hard time believing it was over. "Are you sure you feel up to it?"

She gave him a crooked smile. "I know I look rough, but I feel fine." She tilted her head to the side. "Come on. I've been locked up the last two days." Her voice took on a pleading tone. But there was nothing annoying about it. Paige didn't do whiny or cajoling. Instead, her voice was low and sweet and sincere. How was he supposed to resist that?

"Okay." He couldn't keep her sealed up forever. Someday he was going to have to trust that it was, in fact, over.

For the next several minutes, she held the phone in front of her, alternating between tapping and scrolling. Finally, she stopped. "Chevelle's. It's a sports-themed restaurant. Looks like good food and a fun atmosphere."

"Chevelle's it is. Go ahead and map it."

A few minutes later, he pulled into a parking space along Valley River Avenue, three spaces down from the front door. He killed the engine and glanced around, even though he'd been surveying his surroundings since leaving the jail. Vigilance was a hard habit to break.

After helping Paige from the passenger side, he walked her inside. She was right about it being a fun atmosphere, with its eclectic decor and lighthearted signs, like Hippies Use Side Door. When the hostess seated them, he folded his hands on the checkered table-cloth. Multiple windows let in the late-afternoon light. They left him feeling too exposed to fully relax.

Paige wasn't having that problem. She was leaning back in her chair, wearing a crooked smile. Maybe it was relief, knowing she'd escaped a jail sentence. Or maybe it was thinking her ordeal was over.

After the waitress took their orders, he drew in a deep breath and tried to shake off the tension. Paige was right. Blanton had been the one looking for them in the woods and was behind the other attacks she mentioned. He was probably the one wielding the baseball bat, too.

Tanner drew in a sudden breath. There was one thing he hadn't checked. "I need to find out what kind of car Blanton drives."

"Why?"

"If it doesn't match the description of the car that followed us into Bryson City, we've got a problem."

"I bet it will. If Blanton was in cahoots with someone else, we would have seen him by now."

After the waitress brought their drinks, Paige took a long sip of tea, then let her hands rest in her lap. "One good thing came out of my getting beat to a pulp. I remembered some things."

"What kind of things?"

"Bits and pieces of my childhood, my life in Orlando. My time at Lowell Correctional Institution." She frowned. "I had a situation like what I just went through. I think it was the similarity of the two that triggered the memory. Or maybe getting knocked in the head again rattled my brains back into place. Members of a rival gang had set out to kill me, and it was a fellow inmate instead of a CO who came to my rescue."

"A member of your gang?"

The waitress placed a basket of bread in front of them, and Paige slathered butter on a piece. "No, Iris didn't belong to a gang. That can be dangerous. But she was big enough, no one messed with her. Six feet two inches of solid muscle. She's doing life for murder, but she's a changed person. Found God in prison, was always talking about how He'd changed her life. A few people listened. Most of us just wanted her to shut up."

Paige shook her head. "At a whole foot shorter and a hundred pounds lighter, I wasn't dumb enough to physically threaten her, but I gave her a lot of grief."

"But she defended you when you got attacked?"

She nodded. "I thought I was going to die. When I woke up in the hospital a couple days later and learned what she'd done, I decided I wanted Iris to be my role model, right down to serving the God she served. It's been a long road. I've had a lifetime of bad habits to overcome, and I'm still not there."

Yeah, he knew all about the requirements. And he wasn't even trying. What was the use? He'd never be able to live up to those standards. God wanted the "good" kids. That was what they'd told him. Maybe they were trying to encourage good behavior. The reasons didn't matter. The God he'd heard about during his childhood would never be interested in him. And that was okay, because Tanner wasn't interested in Him, either.

Paige tore a small piece from the end of her bread. "Before I met Iris, I thought Christianity was just a bunch of rules."

He cocked a brow at her. "That's basically what it is." That, and a platform from which to look down on everyone else.

"If that's all you're seeing, you're looking at a counterfeit. It's not about rules. It's about a relationship. Even with the holes I still have in my memory, when I compare my life without God to my life with God, the benefits far outweigh the sacrifices. I've traded addiction for victory, hatred for love, emptiness for a life that's full and satisfying."

She laid her bread down to take a swig of tea. "Anyway, when I got out, I knew I needed to make a fresh start and go where no one knew me. Not only would it be dangerous to stay, I didn't want to risk getting sucked back into that old lifestyle. So I headed to Atlanta."

"That must have been hard."

"Not really. My mom died of a drug overdose when I was seventeen, and I never knew my dad. My only friends were in the gang and would've tried to kill me if they knew I wanted out."

"So, you had no one." The thought of Paige facing an unknown future alone brought up another image, the one that often invaded his sleep—an eight-year-old boy being whisked out of the only home he remembered, the bloody bodies of his mother and sister still inside.

She shrugged. "I had my brother."

"You remember him now?"

"I remember growing up together, and I remember him coming to visit me at the prison. Being seven years older, I pretty much raised him. Our mom was usually too strung out on her current drug of choice."

"I know what it's like." They were kindred spirits. It was something he'd felt almost from the beginning, that underlying bond that comes through shared trauma.

An odd sadness settled over him. Paige's remembering her past was what they'd hoped for. But it meant she'd soon leave. Life wasn't going to be the same without her. He'd spent every day with her almost since he'd gotten to Murphy.

When their salads arrived, she picked at hers, head

down. "Tommy always idolized me. Followed me right into a life of crime. Didn't follow me back out." She stabbed a forkful of greens. "Now he's dead."

Guilt bore down on her, and she curled her shoulders forward. He understood that, too. The crushing burden of being responsible for someone else's death. How could he help her when he hadn't figured out how to help himself?

He laid down his fork and reached across the table to cover her hand with his. "You know, everyone chooses their own path."

"Some paths are more like trenches, with steep, slippery slopes. I can't stop feeling like I put him there."

"You were on the same path, and you climbed out of it."

"I had Iris."

"And Tommy had you. You brought him to Atlanta with you, right? He had every opportunity to turn his life around. But he chose the other path. Different city, same old stuff. If you hadn't gotten into trouble, he'd have probably followed someone who had."

"Thank you." She withdrew her hand and sucked in a deep breath. "When I got out of jail, Tommy met me with a bag of stuff he'd hung on to for me. We hitched a ride with a trucker and were in Atlanta by daybreak the next day. After two nights sleeping on park benches, we got help from an inner-city mission. Now I waitress in a mom-and-pop place and spend my spare time volunteering with the same mission that helped me get on my feet."

Admiration swelled inside. She was his complement in every way. She enjoyed the same activities he did, but it went deeper than that. They'd shared the same dysfunctional upbringing and understood the scars it left. And they were both working to move beyond their past traumas.

She stabbed a tomato, then let it hover above her plate. "I've developed some friendships with the other volunteers at the mission, but it's the work itself that really fills a void for me. I work with first, second and third graders in an after-school program." Her lips curved up in a soft smile, and every last trace of tension left her features. This was Paige with her guard down, walls gone. Whether from relief or security or some kind of God-given peace, he'd take it.

Her smile widened. "Kids are awesome. Though they've been touched by the ugliness of life, that childish innocence still shines through. A little love can make a lot of difference in their lives."

"And you have a lot to give." He could see that now. With each new memory, she was discovering herself. He was discovering her, too. And he liked what he saw.

She pulled in a long, slow breath. "Shortly after I got to Atlanta, I ran into someone from the old neighborhood. Jake. I thought sure he was going to rat me out. But he'd had his own wake-up call, and since he had family in Atlanta, that's where he ended up. We've gotten really close. He's even been volunteering with me at the mission."

Maybe it was Jake's ring she'd worn. His chest tightened, and he scolded himself. Paige would make a great friend, but that was as far as either of them would let it go.

She frowned. "Recently, I've been afraid he's slipping backward, though."

"Getting back into drugs?"

"Yeah. Some other stuff, too. His brother got out of jail not too long ago, and he's really bad news. I'm worried about the influence he's having on Jake."

Maybe it *had* been Jake's ring and that was why she'd taken it off. If he got back on the right track, the ring might go right back on Paige's finger.

She gave him a sad smile. "It doesn't help that he's been spending a lot of time with my brother, too. Whenever I get back, he's going to be my first project. Sometimes people need some accountability, someone to care enough to show them some tough love."

"Just be careful."

"Don't worry. Jake's harmless."

He laid his fork across his empty salad plate. "Any more recent memories about your brother?"

"That's still a total blank. I don't know what he did, why he was on the Appalachian Trail with me or why Blanton killed him." She shook her head. "My brain feels like swiss cheese. I think the really traumatic events are stored in the holes, way down at the bottom."

"Those will come back, too. It's just taking a little longer."

By the time they finished their meal, the sky around Nantahala Bank next door had turned vibrant shades of orange, pink and lavender. He led Paige to the door, then walked out ahead of her. After glancing up and down the sidewalk and scanning the businesses across the street, he tilted his head, indicating for her to follow.

She smiled as she stepped out onto the sidewalk. "You're still in bodyguard mode."

"And I will be until I check out Blanton's car."

As he led her past the SUV two spaces down from his, a sense of uneasiness crept through him. He picked up his pace and glanced across the street again. He'd positioned her between him and the building, so she was somewhat shielded by his body. But if someone was in front or behind...

They'd almost reached the truck when movement ahead drew his attention. A figure had stepped out from behind the Nantahala Bank sign.

Low-hanging tree branches covered the upper portion of the body. Jeans-clad legs ended in tennis shoes spread shoulder width apart, one foot slightly behind the other. A fraction of a second later, the branches moved, creating a small opening.

In one smooth motion, Tanner grabbed Paige, spun 180 degrees and dived between his vehicle and the next one. A soft *pfsst* whizzed through the air, and they hit the pavement with a thud and a cry from Paige.

"What are you doing?" Her voice was raised, her tone tinged with shock and pain.

Anger drove his volume. "Someone just shot at us."

"I didn't hear anything."

He pulled his phone from his pocket, continuing to scan the area. Since he'd taken the last parking space, he had an unobstructed view beneath his truck. "They used a pistol with a silencer."

His hand shook as he pulled up the keypad and dialed the numbers. "When I said we needed to eat in the room, you should have listened." He ground out the words. "You could've been killed."

"And it wouldn't have been your fault."

"I promised to protect you."

The dispatcher came on at the same moment an engine roared to life a short distance away.

"We're in front of Chevelle's. Someone just shot at

us." As he spoke, the roar grew closer. A car barreled toward them.

He dropped his phone to the pavement and gave Paige a shove. "Get under the truck."

As the car passed behind them, he rose and leaped around the front bumper, pistol raised. The driver fired another shot. Glass shattered.

Tanner didn't have the opportunity to discharge his own weapon. The car sped past and disappeared around the first corner.

He cast a glance over his shoulder. Cracks fanned out from a hole in the center of the large window. Inside Chevelle's, several patrons faced them with wide eyes and lax jaws, but no one looked hurt.

Tanner dropped to his knees beside the truck. "Are you okay?"

"I'm fine."

She crawled out from her hiding place, and he picked up the phone. The dispatcher was still there.

He shoved the phone Paige's direction. "Get in the truck and fill her in. We're going after him."

When he climbed into the driver's seat, Paige was relaying the incident to the dispatcher. They had no description of the shooter beyond blue jeans, dark sneakers and a dark shirt. But he was pretty sure the vehicle was the same one that had followed them into Bryson City.

"Tell them to be on the lookout for an older car, boxy model, lighter color."

He made a right onto Church Street, but the car was gone. While he continued to search, Paige remained on the phone, ready to relay the location should they spot the car.

Finally, the dispatcher gave Paige the news he'd been

waiting for. Police had stopped a light-colored older-model Lincoln headed west out of Murphy. A pistol with a silencer lay on the front-passenger floorboard. The driver was in custody.

Paige disconnected the call, and Tanner drove back to Chevelle's to give a report. A few minutes later, a Murphy police cruiser turned between the restaurant and the bank and stopped in one of the parking spaces against the building.

The uniformed officer stepped out and introduced himself. He was maybe five years Tanner's senior and exuded the warmth and friendliness of someone whose job consisted more of serving the community than dealing with the dregs of society. In another week and a half, Tanner would be welcomed into the family.

A customer had already retrieved the bullet before they arrived. After taking it into evidence, the officer interviewed him and Paige. The suspect was a man by the name of Dylan Hargrave, street name Bruno. Paige didn't know him.

As soon as they were free to go, Tanner headed toward the Hampton Inn to let Paige gather her belongings.

She heaved a long sigh. "It's finally over."

"I think you might be right." Both men involved in her brother's murder were behind bars. Or soon would be.

He parked in front of the Hampton Inn and, for the first time, walked to the door without looking over his shoulder. When they stepped into the room and closed the door, Paige stood in front of him, frowning.

"Tell me why you reacted so strongly tonight."

His jaw dropped. "Why I reacted to someone trying to kill us?"

"No, why you got so angry with me. I said I didn't want to be cooped up in the hotel room for dinner, and you went along with it. Then when things didn't go like you thought, you were furious with me." She narrowed her eyes. "There's someone in your life that you failed to protect. And you've been paying for it ever since."

"That's ridiculous."

"Who is it?" Her eyes filled with disbelief. "It's your sister, isn't it? You blame yourself for your sister's death."

A weight settled in his gut, a lead-filled balloon. It grew heavier, expanding till it hurt.

Paige put a hand on his arm. "I talked to you about my brother. You listened. Just sharing made me feel a little better. Talk to me, Tanner. Let me help you."

"It's not the same."

"It doesn't matter. Everything's easier when you share it with someone."

He closed his eyes against the memories surging forward. Paige was wrong. Sharing wouldn't make it easier.

She stepped closer and clutched his other arm. A faint scent wafted upward, a subtle hint of mint with something fruity, and he fought the urge to bury his face in her hair. When she spoke, her voice was husky. "Your sister's death wasn't any more your fault than my brother's was mine."

Yes, it was. He tightened his hands into fists. "I was a coward." The words were the softest whisper. At first, he wasn't sure he'd said them aloud.

"You were a child."

"So was she."

"Tell me what happened."

No. He'd never given anyone the details. Not the police. Not the social workers. Not even Colton and Bryce.

He opened his eyes, a refusal ready on his lips. Then his gaze collided with hers. Compassion filled her dark eyes, along with a silent plea. It tugged at him, an invisible cord born of shared trauma. She'd understand him on a level no one else could. Spending the evening with her, guard down, walls gone, had sent a constant barrage of cannonballs at his defenses. The last of his reservations shattered, the shards mixed with the rubble of his own walls.

"It was late." The semimonotone belied the emotion churning within. "Teri and I shared a small room with a double bed. Shouts woke us up. My mom's boyfriend was drunk and beating on her. That was a regular occurrence, but this time was worse. Teri locked the door and got back into bed."

And she'd held him, like she always did when the fights erupted, telling him it was going to be okay. But she'd been wrong. It hadn't been okay.

"We heard a gunshot, and everything went quiet. Teri unlocked the window. But it wouldn't lift. I'd never seen that window open." Even in the summertime. The small AC unit in the living room had never been powerful enough to send much air into the bedroom, so on those weeks when temperatures climbed into the high eighties and low nineties, they'd toughed it out.

"We heard footsteps in the hall, and she worked even harder on the window." He started to turn away, but Paige's grip on his arms tightened. He heaved a sigh.

"You know what I was doing? Lying in bed, too scared to move." Disgust laced his words.

Her eyebrows drew together, making deep vertical lines between them. "You were what, eleven? Ten?"

"Eight."

"What do you think you could have done?"

"Helped her open the window, so we could have both escaped."

"There's a reason you never saw that window open. It was probably jammed or painted shut. If your mother couldn't do it, do you really think you could have made a difference?"

She was probably right. But he'd been beating himself up for too many years to let it go that easily.

"He started pounding on the door, demanding we open it. Then he kicked it. Teri yanked me up and shoved me under the bed. I heard another kick, and the door crashed open."

He swallowed against the bile pushing its way up his throat. "There was a gunshot, and Teri fell beside the bed. She had her finger in front of her lips, warning me to not make a sound. She saved my life and gave her own in the process." He dropped his head. "And I did nothing."

"Anything you could have done would have gotten you killed, too. You would've died and still wouldn't have been able to save your sister. You lived, due to the quick thinking of a twelve-year-old. Appreciate the gift you've been given."

She released him, then wrapped both arms around his waist. "Let yourself heal. Let God help you heal."

She tightened her grip, her head nestled beneath his chin, the side of her face resting against his chest. He dipped his head and pressed his lips to her hair, breathing in her scent. She was only offering comfort. He needed to remember that.

But she felt so good in his arms. She was a balm for his tortured soul, the cure for his loneliness, healing salve over the guilt he'd carried for so long.

When she finally pulled away, he held on a second longer before letting her go.

She'd said to appreciate the gift he'd been given. He'd never considered his life a gift. He'd been too focused on what he'd lost. His home, dumpy as it was. His mother, who had her faults but still loved him. His sweet, gentle sister. Maybe he'd been focusing on the wrong things. Could he learn to think of his life as a blessing?

If he did, it would probably change a lot of things.

First, he'd have to let go of the anger he'd carried for so long—with circumstances, with the man who killed his family and, most of all, with God.

He couldn't be grateful and still be angry.

Because gratitude and anger never went hand in hand.

NINE

Paige stared down at her phone where information on Millie's Place was displayed. According to the tagline, it promised great Southern cooking.

This was the mom-and-pop diner where she worked. Or had before she disappeared for the past week and a half. If Millie had found someone else, Paige wouldn't blame her.

After getting back to Tanner's last night, she'd decided it was time to go home. Tanner wasn't happy. He wanted her to stay in Murphy until she'd regained all her memories. But she had enough. She knew where she worked, and Millie would have her address. She'd also have her banking information on the back of any paychecks she'd cashed.

She pressed the green phone icon and listened through two rings. When a sweet female voice answered, a rush of emotion flooded her.

Millie was the mother she'd never had. When no one else had wanted to hire someone fresh out of jail, Millie had been willing to give her a chance. Two days later, she'd given her full access to the cash register.

"Hi, Millie. It's Paige." She closed her eyes. Soon she'd know whether she still had a job.

"I didn't expect to hear from you till Friday. Are you at a checkpoint, or did you head back early?"

Paige opened her eyes. She was still on vacation. Her job was safe. "I headed back early."

"I'm glad. I didn't like the idea of you doing a three-week hike all alone. You're a tough girl, but there's too many crazies out there."

Millie went on to chat about things going on at the restaurant, but Paige's brain had gotten stuck on the word *alone*. If she was doing the trip alone, how did she end up with Thomas?

She pulled her attention back to Millie's conversation, the murmur of voices and clang of dishes a chaotic backdrop. The restaurant was busy with the lunch crowd.

"Enough chatter from me. How was your trip?"

"It was… I'm not sure." Paige swallowed hard. She needed to tell Millie what had happened. She'd know something was wrong as soon as Paige returned to work. More important, she might be able to fill in some holes. "I fell. Hit my head. My memory is…a little foggy."

"Oh, no. Are you all right?"

"I will be." She had no doubt. God had been with her every step of the way. "Did I tell you how I was getting to the trail?" She'd probably left her car somewhere and needed to find it.

"You were going to a friend's house, someone who used to work at the mission. She was going to drive you there the next morning. You'd planned to hike as far north as you could, then catch a bus home. That was going to be Friday, so you could be back at work on Saturday."

"I'll be there. What time?"

"Six a.m."

"Also…" Paige closed her eyes again. If this didn't worry Millie, nothing would. "Can you give me my address?"

"You don't remember where you live?" Millie's pitch was several notes higher than normal. "Paige Tatem, have you seen a doctor?"

"Yes. It's just a little amnesia. The doctor assured me my memory would return with time." Each day she was remembering more.

Last night, it had been with the aid of another nightmare. Once again, she'd watched her brother's murder. But this time there'd been two men. Blanton had given his commands while the other walked silently, exuding a sense of calm control. When Tommy had told them what they wanted to know, the quiet one had raised his weapon and fired.

But there was more—a tattoo on the upper part of his back—triangles, squares and rectangles poking out over the top of his sweatshirt. She was 99 percent sure the man in her dream was the same one the police captured last night. A simple call to Murphy PD to inquire about tattoos would eliminate the 1 percent.

There was rustling on the other end of the line as Millie returned to the phone. "All right, I've got it."

Paige jotted down the address. "One more thing." If she was going to worry her boss, she might as well go all out. "Can you tell me what kind of car I drive?"

Millie huffed out an exasperated sigh. "When you

get back, I'm taking you to *my* doctor. Ford Focus. Red. A little beat-up. Maybe 2007 or 2008."

Paige thanked her, promising to see her in four days, then disconnected the call.

Four days. If she hoped to be at Millie's at 6:00 a.m. on Saturday morning, she needed to be home no later than Friday. Tomorrow or Thursday would be even better. She had a lot to do to get settled.

She clutched the phone to her chest. She'd known the day was coming when she'd regain her memory and return to her old life. It was what she'd looked forward to. Now she wasn't so sure.

Good grief, what was wrong with her? She was totally mixed-up, and it had nothing to do with lack of memory.

But it was no wonder. Tanner had saved her life. Several times. Victims often fell in love with their rescuers. There was probably even a name for it in some psychological journal.

Whoa, back up. Love? No, that wasn't what she meant. She'd regained enough of her memory to know that no man was getting past her defenses that easily.

She laid the phone on the small kitchen table and paused, left hand outstretched. That lighter band of skin around her ring finger represented one of those holes in her swiss-cheese brain. Someone had loved her enough to ask her to marry him. And she'd loved him enough to say yes. So why couldn't she remember him?

She curled her fingers into a fist and straightened them again. What kind of ring had she worn and who'd given it to her? She closed her eyes and pulled up an image—a single diamond in a simple gold band. Or maybe it was flanked by two baguettes. Or maybe the band was white gold.

She opened her eyes. It was no use. She couldn't remember the ring any better than she could remember the man who'd given it to her. Maybe if she could recall the one, she'd have the other. She sank into the chair, still staring at her hand.

A memory stirred, then came into sharp focus. A flat silver band a quarter-inch wide. It wasn't an engagement ring. A cross stretched along one-third of the circumference, punched all the way through the thickness of the metal.

Millie had given it to her after one month on her new job. It was to remind her of the commitment she made in prison. Anytime she was tempted to return to her old life, she was to look at the ring and remember God's promise to never leave her and her own promise to always love Him. She'd taken off the ring and left it at home rather than risk losing it on the trail.

A sense of relief swept through her. There was no man waiting for her at home. The moment she saw Tanner, she'd let him know.

Her heart fluttered. Last night, something had changed. As they'd stood in her hotel room, the barriers between them had come down. Maybe those walls had been only on her end. But his opening up and trusting her with his pain had blasted holes in all her defenses.

And when she'd held him and he'd hugged her back, she'd felt as if she'd come home. In his arms was where she belonged. Now that she knew she was unattached, maybe they could…

No, Tanner didn't think of her like that. She was no longer in danger, so they'd transitioned from victim and protector to friends. That was all. If he had any desire for more than that, she'd have known by now.

Her phone buzzed with an incoming text. It was Tanner, letting her know lunch was ready. After shooting off a response, she slid her phone into one pocket, then stuffed the paper with her address into another.

When she walked in his back door, the table was already set, and Tanner was placing a casserole dish in the center. The noon news drifted in from the next room.

She drew in a fragrant breath, then frowned. "I was supposed to be cooking for you to help earn my keep. That didn't work out well."

"Considering you spent most of that time sealed up in a hotel room, you have an excuse."

She took a seat at the table. "I need to go home tomorrow. I'm scheduled to work Saturday and have a lot to accomplish before then."

His smile faded, and her heart stuttered at the disappointment on his face. No, that wasn't disappointment. It was concern. He didn't want her going home until she'd fully regained her memory. Once sure she was safe, he'd deposit her in Atlanta with no regrets.

"I remember more of my past. And I now know where I live." She pulled the sheet of paper from her pocket, then smoothed it out on the table. "This is my address. My car is apparently at a friend's house."

"How will you get to work?"

"MARTA, Atlanta's transit system. Or maybe it's close enough to walk." She removed her phone from her other pocket. After bringing up Millie's Place, she mapped the distance to home. "A mile and a half. Until I find my car, I'll walk it."

His brows drew together. "That's too far."

"If I'm fit enough to hike the Appalachian Trail, I think I can handle a mile and a half on sidewalks."

"That's not what I mean. I don't know what your new place is like, but where you used to live is downright scary. You could get mugged, especially coming home in the dark."

"Millie's only serves breakfast and lunch, so I won't be coming home in the dark." She'd be leaving home before sunup, but she wouldn't mention that.

She watched Tanner set a glass of iced tea at each place and take a seat opposite her. "I remember the ring."

His gaze shot to her face. "You do?"

"A silver band with a cross cut into it. Millie gave it to me. I took it off so I wouldn't lose it."

"It wasn't an engagement ring."

His tone held relief. The smile that spread across his face did funny things to her insides. Maybe she'd been wrong and Tanner wanted more than friendship, something they were now free to pursue. Why else would the news make him happy?

She matched his smile with one of her own. "I'm not engaged. Or recently unengaged."

His smile dimmed several watts, and he nodded, the motion abrupt. Something had changed, as quickly as a switch being flipped. "That's good. At least we know you're not going home to a crazed ex-fiancé. You know what they say about a lover spurned."

Her hopes crashed down around her. She should've known. Tanner was a cop, and cops didn't hook up with women who had pasts as stained as hers. He was only concerned for her safety. With Tanner, everything went back to her safety.

After bowing her head to offer thanks, she looked up at him. "When I leave, I hope we can stay in touch."

He nodded. "I'd like that."

"If you're on Facebook, I'll send you a friend request."

"I'll accept it."

A stiffness had entered their conversation. She scooped up a bite and blew on it.

"Are you okay?"

His question caught her off guard. "Fine. Why?"

"You seem like something's bothering you."

"Everything's fine." Except that she was leaving and really wanted Tanner to ask her to stay, but he wouldn't, because he didn't feel the same way about her that she felt about him. And there was no way she was going to tell him that.

He still watched her. "You don't open up to people easily, do you?"

She shrugged. "Trust isn't easy for me."

"Isn't trust something you have to have to be a Christian?"

"I trust God. It's people I have a problem with."

"Are you really trusting God if you won't let anyone get close to you?"

Heat built in her chest. Was he judging her? "Maybe I've figured out that God is the only one I *can* trust. Because you know what I've remembered so far?" She pushed her chair out and stood. "I remember my first trip to jail. My boyfriend set me up. He figured I might get a lighter sentence, so he'd just let me pay for his crime." She strode across the kitchen and back again. "And I remember my best friend coming to live with me when I was trying to get on my feet between jail terms and stealing my rent money. And I remember, at ten years old, walking to a neighborhood a mile away and weeding flower beds for two dollars an hour so that I could buy food for Tommy and me, and my mother finding the money and spending it on drugs." Which had led Paige to steal the old lady's purse. "And then there's my brother, who threw me under the bus more times than I can count." She sliced the air with one hand. "So yes, I think I have a few trust issues."

She plopped into the chair. In the next room, the newscaster launched into a new story—a woman found murdered in her home in Jasper, Georgia.

Jasper. It was off 575. They'd driven through it on their way to and from Atlanta. But it was more than that. It meant something to her.

Tanner picked up the salt and shook it over his plate. "I'm sorry—"

She held up a hand, cutting off his apology.

What was significant about Jasper?

"Paige?"

She rose from the chair and walked into the living room. A reporter stood in front of a middle-class, ranch-style home. A UPS driver had tried to deliver a package that morning and discovered a foul odor coming from inside the house. The woman had been dead for some time, shot in the head.

"Do you know her?"

"I don't know. I feel like I know someone in Jasper."

She returned her attention to the TV. Authorities were withholding the name of the victim until they could notify next of kin. If seeing the house didn't help her, hearing the name probably wouldn't, either.

The camera cut back to the studio, where the anchors promised updates as soon as they became available.

Paige's thoughts churned. Why did it feel as if she should remember the place? As if that death was somehow connected to her?

She retrieved her phone from the table and pressed the Google Microphone icon. "Where does the Appalachian Trail begin in the South?"

Within moments she had her answer. The trail began at Springer Mountain. She returned to the living room, and a little further searching told her something else: Jasper was thirty minutes away.

She put a hand over her mouth and sank onto the couch.

Tanner sat next to her. "What is it?"

Before she could answer, the camera cut back to the scene. The police had just discovered a car hidden in the woods. If it was hidden, it couldn't be hers. She'd have parked in the driveway.

The dead woman couldn't be her friend.

Then the camera panned over the car. She released a strangled gasp. It was a red Ford Focus.

"That's my car. I don't know why it's in the woods, but before I left, I told Millie I was spending the night with a friend, and she was dropping me off at the trailhead the next morning."

Which meant her prints would be all over the house.

Paige put her head back against the couch and released a moan. More evidence against her. Hiding her car in the woods instead of parking in plain view made her look even more guilty.

Why would she do that? And where did Thomas play into this whole scenario?

She needed to get the rest of her memory back. The sooner the better.

Preferably before the police questioned her about this newest murder.

Tanner strolled down a paved path leading toward the river's edge. The sun was well into its ascent and had chased away the morning chill sometime ago.

Paige walked next to him, her pace relaxed. But tension emanated from her. Yesterday afternoon, he'd driven her to Jasper and they'd told the police what they knew. Crime scene investigators were still processing her car. Besides lifting prints and taking hair and DNA samples, they'd found a tracking device, which helped to shift some of the suspicion off her. The killer had likely followed her to Jasper.

She lifted her shoulders and let them fall, the motion seeming to shake off some of the tension. Yesterday afternoon, they'd contacted Murphy PD about Hargrave's tattoos. This morning they'd received an answer. He had lots of them, including a complicated geometric pattern that covered most of his upper back. Unfortunately, Paige couldn't say for sure whether the photos in the database matched what she remembered from her dream. Tanner would've preferred 100 percent certainty.

Paige released a sigh. "I'm glad you brought me here. I hate to leave Murphy without getting to see something besides the inside of my hotel room."

"I'm glad Colton suggested it."

She'd decided to stay in Murphy until Thursday or Friday, hoping she'd be able to pick up her car on her way to Atlanta. Since he had an extra day or two with her, Tanner had asked his friend for advice. Knowing Paige's love for nature, Colton had recommended Konehete Park in downtown Murphy.

Paige kicked a twig off the path and into the grass. "Tommy was the one who drove my car to my friend's house. I remember now. He insisted on pulling it into the woods so it'd be out of the way."

Tanner nodded. The car being hidden, the tracking device. Now it made sense. Since Paige and Tommy weren't there when the woman was shot, the killers probably arrived after she'd taken them to the trailhead. She may have even told them where they'd gone, figuring she'd alert Paige, then never got the chance.

Paige released a sigh. "I've spent the last year trying to keep him out of trouble. He was finally doing well, had even landed a decent job the week before I left. But he needed transportation. He said if he could borrow the Focus, he'd have the money to buy his own when I got back. It was going to be sitting idle for three weeks, so I figured, *why not?* I walked to work those last few days, then had him drop me off at my friend's house."

"How'd he end up with you on the trail?"

"Late that night, I got a call from him. He said he'd lost the job, but that it wasn't his fault." She rolled her eyes. "Nothing was ever my brother's fault."

Tanner flashed her a sympathetic smile. "With people like that, it usually isn't."

"He said he was bummed and wanted to go hiking with me. I tried to discourage him. Tommy was into playing video games and hanging out with friends. I knew he'd never make it. But he kept bugging me. I finally said he could go, on two conditions—that he kept up with me and didn't mouth a single word of complaint."

"How did he do?"

"Really well, actually. He was so winded a few times, I thought he was going to keel over. But he kept moving. Now I know why."

"Those guys were coming after him." Tanner shook his head. Thomas had ticked off some really bad dudes, then led them to his sister. The man was lower than pond scum. The world was better off without him.

Paige crossed her arms and walked in silence, jaw tight. Ahead, a swing hung from a wooden frame near the water's edge. When they reached it, Paige stepped off the path to sit, and he joined her.

She released a soft sigh. "This is pretty."

"It is." Colton had done well. Poplar trees shaded where they sat, and the river moved lazily in front of them. All around, expanses of lawn were beginning to green up for spring.

But a sense of melancholy seemed to have settled over her. The excitement he expected wasn't there. She was going home. To the job she claimed to enjoy. To her volunteer work that she found so fulfilling.

When she'd told him yesterday that she remembered the ring, he'd waited with bated breath. Upon learning she wasn't engaged, he'd wanted to give a victory shout. Then reason trumped fantasy, and he explained away his relief with the spurned lover comment. She'd seemed disappointed. Maybe even hurt. Was it possible she'd fallen for him and now didn't want to leave?

Conflicting emotions collided within him. One part of him wanted to ask her to stay, to allow them to spend time together, to enjoy each other's company without any threats and explore the possibilities of a future together. That was the side of him that envied what Colton and Mandy had, the part that lay awake, longing for a soul mate to help fill the emptiness that crept through him in the wee hours of the morning.

The other part of him knew he needed to let her go. That was the sensible, rational side that made decisions based on a list of pros and cons and well-thought-out arguments. Ever since he found her in the woods, he'd tried to do what was best for her. And letting her go was best, no matter what he felt.

He glanced over at her. She sat staring across the water, into the greenery on the opposite bank. She was an amazing woman. But she was broken. She had to be. No one could go through a childhood like hers and come out whole. She needed someone solid enough to provide the stable home she'd never had. A rock.

That wasn't him. His childhood was as messed up as hers. He simply wasn't relationship material, and he had a short string of failed ones to prove it. Brittney was the latest of four.

He breathed in the earthy scent of the riverbank and let the swaying motion of the swing soothe some of his tension. Thoughts of Brittney always left him feeling agitated. Thinking about his other exes did, too. He'd never handled failure well.

He didn't even know what he'd done wrong. He had no clue what went into building a successful relationship. He'd never had one modeled. Maybe in a couple of the foster homes. But those stays had been too brief for anything to stick. No matter his intentions, he'd never be able to provide a woman with what she needed on an emotional level.

Beside him, Paige released a soft sigh. "When I leave, I hope you'll try to find a church."

One corner of his mouth twitched up. From exes to church. Paige's thoughts hadn't been traveling on the same path as his. "I wouldn't have to find one. Colton's been inviting me to his since I arrived."

"Good."

"I don't know how good it is." He frowned. "I doubt God wants much to do with me. I've spent most of my life angry at Him." Paige had given him a lot to think about at the hotel. But change like that didn't happen overnight.

She gave him a playful elbow jab. "God isn't scared off by your anger. Do you have any idea how many times I cursed Him growing up?" She turned in the swing to face him more fully. "I can tell you all about anger. I used to have a temper that was scary. Blanton might say I still do." She flashed him a crooked grin. "That first memory I had? I turned down the guy's advances and he insulted me. I jumped him, knocked him down and told him if he ever dissed me again, I'd carve his heart out with a butter knife. Does that sound like someone God would want on His team?"

No, but apparently, He did. And Tanner found that encouraging in a way he never expected. All he'd witnessed growing up were "perfect" people with their holier-than-thou attitudes. Paige was different. She was guarded but humble. And she was far from perfect. If Paige had found it, maybe a relationship with God wasn't out of reach for him after all.

"What do you say we see the rest of this park?" She rose from the swing.

He stood to walk with her. "Are you sure you're ready to go home this week?" The longer he could keep her in Murphy, the better he'd feel. She wasn't fully recovered. What if those final missing memories let her walk into something dangerous?

"I'd better be. I'm reporting to work Saturday."

"If you're not ready, I'm sure Millie would hold your job."

"I'll be fine."

Ahead, the path forked, the left-hand branch moving away from the water. Some kind of monument stood in the Y. When they reached it, Paige stopped.

"I remember the box. It was mine."

He lifted his brows. "It didn't belong to Thomas?"

"He stole it from me." She crossed her arms, her jaw tight. "All the times I've held it, straining to remember. This morning when I went to pack it, it all came back to me. Ms. Collins, my fourth-grade teacher, gave it to me, with a pewter star tucked into the main drawer. She said I had potential, and that star represented my dreams. I didn't know what *potential* was, but both the box and the trinket meant a lot to me."

She stared down at the memorial in front of her, placed there by the Cherokee County Chapter of The Compassionate Friends. A stone angel wrapped a heart engraved with the words *This Monument Dedicated in Memory of Our Children*. A pillar on each side commemorated those who had died over the years. But Paige didn't seem to be reading any of the dozens of names listed there.

"We stopped for lunch. When he pulled his canteen out of his pack, the box fell out. I couldn't believe he'd taken it. When I saw my pewter star was gone and he had joints in there instead, I went nuts, ripped them up and scattered the pot."

"That's how the remnants ended up in the drawer."

"Yeah. I was furious. Not only had he stolen from me, but he'd been playing me all this time." Her hand shook as she tucked her hair behind her ear. "I blasted him, grabbed both canteens to fill and left him on the trail with our packs. While I was gone, the killers showed up."

His heart fell. That meant the last words she'd spoken to him were in anger.

"On my way back, I heard loud voices. My brother's had an edge of panic. Apparently there'd been a drug deal and things had gone wrong. Gunfire broke out. In the confusion, Tommy took off with both the cash and the heroin."

Tanner shook his head. "Not a smart decision."

"My brother wasn't known for smart decisions." She frowned, then continued, "The guys weren't happy about it. They made him walk into the woods. I followed. Finally, they stopped a few yards up from a creek and demanded to know what he'd done with the drugs and money. He said everything was in a duffel bag in his storage unit, that I had the key and the code and had just gone to get water."

Tanner's jaw tightened. Yeah, definitely pond scum.

Her eyes glistened with unshed tears. "They shot him and kicked his body down the hill and into the creek."

He looped an arm around her shoulders and pulled her against his side. "I'm sorry you had to see that."

"Thanks. But I think that box saved my life. If he hadn't stolen it, I wouldn't have gone off alone, and I'd probably be dead."

"God works in mysterious ways." He stifled a smile. Did he just give a quote about God? Maybe Paige's words were sinking in.

She began walking again, and he let his arm fall from her shoulders. They had a friendship where a comforting hug was appropriate, not a stroll-through-the-park-arm-in-arm kind of relationship.

"So how did Tommy get the box to begin with?"

"He helped me move. Twice. When my lease was up at the apartment, I temporarily moved in with a friend from work and put my things in storage. A month later, I got my own place, and Tommy helped me move again."

"And decided to keep some of your stuff."

"This wasn't the first time he'd stolen from me. I tried to keep an eye on him, but I guess I didn't do so well. Anyway, he asked if he could take over my storage unit. One of the volunteers at the mission was moving out of state and getting rid of a lot of his stuff. Tommy wanted to sell some and keep the rest. Guess he decided to make that storage unit even more lucrative." She rolled her eyes. "On the last trip, we fitted everything into my car except three boxes of books. I never got around to getting them. Tommy insisted they weren't in his way."

"I'm sure he did." More things to identify the unit as his sister's if he got caught.

She stopped to watch a group of ducks at the water's edge. "I guess it's time to put everything behind me. I have my job, my work with the ministry, my friends. One in particular is getting a visit from me as soon as I get back."

"Jake?"

"Yeah."

He drew in a slow breath, trying to ease a sudden tightness in his chest. "I wish you'd let me go with you."

She flashed him a *get real* look. "I'm hoping he'll

open up to me about what's going on in his life. Bringing a cop along isn't the way to get him to talk."

"If he really has gone back to drugs and crime, he won't want you getting in his business."

She smiled, but it didn't do anything to ease his concerns. "I'll be fine. Jake and I are longtime friends. If it'll make you feel better, though, I'll text you when I get home."

"Where does he live?"

"About a mile from me. He lives with his brother in their grandmother's old house."

Tanner frowned. He still didn't like it. "Definitely text me. I won't sleep until you do. I've gotten so used to worrying about you. It's going to be a hard habit to break."

"Thank you." Her smile widened and appreciation filled her eyes. "There aren't many people who'd lose sleep worrying about me."

Based on everything she'd told him about her past, there'd been few people who cared what happened to her, one way or the other.

But he was one of those people and would be for a long time.

Even if it was just as a friend.

Friday arrived much too quickly. Just that morning, Paige had received a call that she could claim her car. As Tanner pulled into the Jasper police station parking lot, his insides tightened.

He replayed the same mental pep talk he'd been giving himself since leaving Murphy. He was happy for her. She was regaining her memory and would soon have her life back. He'd come up with all kinds of reasons why her returning to Atlanta was best. For her anyway.

And it was best for him. He was saving himself the pain of another failed relationship. So why did he feel as if he had a big hole seared through his chest?

He killed the engine. "Are you sure you don't want me to follow you? What if you break down?"

"Then I'll call you."

"Okay. But I'm going inside with you."

He led her into the police station. When they came out twenty minutes later, she'd completed the forms necessary to claim her car. They'd waived the driver's license requirement. She was part of their investigation. They knew who she was.

They'd also given her a key. Besides the tracking device, the detectives had found a spare hidden in a metal box, affixed to the frame with magnets.

When she reached the driver's-side door, she turned to face him. "Thank you for everything you've done. You're getting a big chunk out of my next paycheck and weekly payments thereafter, until I get you repaid."

"Take your time."

She nodded. "You already agreed we're staying in touch, right? Even after I pay you back?"

"Absolutely."

"I'd like to visit North Carolina again soon. Maybe we can go kayaking. If Colton ever lets you replace his." She grinned. "I'd like to experience kayaking the Nantahala without being shot at."

"I don't know. The bullets make it much more exciting."

"I think I've had enough excitement for a while."

Her smile faded, and she stepped toward him. Now

the goodbye. His chest tightened. Sure, they'd promised to stay in touch. But how many such promises evolved into nothing more than infrequent comments on Facebook posts as the demands of life took precedence?

She managed another half smile, but there was sadness behind it. "I can't tell you how much I appreciate everything you've done for me. If you hadn't found me, I wouldn't be alive today."

He shrugged and shifted his weight from one foot to the other. "It was nothing. Like I said before, protecting people is my job."

"And like *I* said before, you've gone way above and beyond. You're a special man, Tanner Brody."

She closed the remaining distance between them and wrapped both arms around his neck. He brought his own up to circle her back. As he held her, warmth flowed through him. Her last words drove deep inside, their message engraved on his soul. *You're a special man, Tanner Brody.* This was the second time she'd told him that.

The last thing he'd ever felt was special. Racked with guilt over his sister's death. Sleep disturbed by nightmares. The kid no one wanted. But Paige felt he was special. Wrapped in her arms, he could almost believe it.

When she finally released him and stepped away, the loss of her warmth left a void that stretched to his core, and he had to steel himself against the cold emptiness creeping in.

She opened the door of the Focus and slid into the driver's seat. "Text me your mailing address. I'll send you the first check as soon as I get paid."

Recouping the money he'd spent was the last thing on his mind, but he nodded anyway. "Text me after your visit with Jake. In fact, text me as soon as you're able to access your apartment."

"I will." She pulled her phone from her purse and started to lay it in the seat. "Uh-oh."

"What?"

"Twelve percent. I should have charged it last night." He frowned at her.

"Hey, I have an excuse for being forgetful." She looked at the charger slot below the dashboard, then opened the glove box. "No car charger. Tommy probably took that, too." She pursed her lips. "I shouldn't accuse him when he's not here to defend himself."

"You're basing your assumptions on a lifetime of experience."

After a final goodbye, she pulled the door shut. He didn't move toward his own vehicle until she disappeared down the street.

As he settled into the driver's seat, he heaved a sigh. He'd never connected with someone as quickly as he had Paige. But the same things that created that special bond also prevented them from having a stable future together. He was too messed up to be what she needed. If they tried, he'd only let her down in the end.

He started his truck and moments later was heading in the opposite direction. It was only noon, which was good. She had a lot to do: gaining access to her apartment, acquiring a copy of the key from the manager, canceling credit cards, getting a new driver's license…

And visiting Jake.

A vise clamped down on his chest. He drew in a deep breath, fighting the tightness.

What was wrong with him? She'd said that she and Jake were just friends. Even if they were more than that, what difference did it make? He'd known from the start that she'd eventually return to her own life.

The miles flew past, and still Paige occupied his thoughts. A sign for Ellijay stood at the edge of the highway. Paige would be nearing the outskirts of Atlanta by now. And the thought of her visiting her old friend still bothered him. It was more than jealousy. It was uneasiness.

People didn't like to be called out on their actions. What if Jake resented her interference?

Then he'd tell her to mind her own business. Or he'd end their friendship. It wouldn't be something to hurt someone over.

When he pulled into his driveway sometime later, he still hadn't been able to put his concerns to rest. He went inside and made himself a sandwich. He'd just finished when a tone notified him of an incoming text.

It was from Paige. The apartment manager had let her in and was having a duplicate key made. Paige was canceling her debit and credit cards, having a quick bite to eat, then getting documentation together for a replacement driver's license.

He sent a text of his own.

Are you charging your phone?

As we speak.

Good. By the time she left, she'd have enough charge to make it through the afternoon. He finished his sandwich, then set to work on washing dishes. Next he'd tackle the lawn. For today, staying busy was a good game plan.

He wheeled the push mower from the shed and gave the rope a couple of sharp yanks. Maybe he'd eventually invest in a rider. But with 80 percent of the two acres being wooded, it seemed pointless.

After finishing the last row, he released the pull-back lever on the handle, and the motor died. Walking the yard pushing a mower was good exercise. Unfortunately, it didn't occupy his mind nearly enough. Because he'd thought of Paige the entire time.

Once inside, he shot off a text: How's it going?

No response.

Over the next fifteen minutes, he checked a dozen times. Three calls also went unanswered.

He laid the phone on the coffee table, his stomach a tangled ball of nerves. If only he knew someone he could ask to check on her. But the only people she'd mentioned by name were Jake and Millie. She wasn't due to show up at Millie's until tomorrow.

And Jake... Tanner had no idea who Jake was, other than someone who'd apparently fallen back into that downward cycle. Someone who Paige was determined to save from his bad choices.

Someone who'd been hanging around with her brother.

What if there was a connection? What if he was involved in whatever had gotten Thomas killed?

Tanner snatched his keys and phone from the coffee table and headed for the door. Paige wouldn't be happy with him. She'd told him not to follow.

But he had a bad feeling. And bad feelings usually had a cause. Even if he didn't know what it was.

He fired up the engine and backed from the drive. The first red light he hit, he would Google Millie's Place and map the route. Paige's apartment was a mile and a half from her job, and Jake lived a mile from her. He'd start at Millie's Place and work outward from there, looking for the red Focus. The search area would cover a maximum radius of two and a half miles.

Yeah, Paige was going to be ticked. But his gut was telling him that she might be walking into something dangerous.

And he never ignored his gut.

TEN

Paige walked toward the rows of plastic chairs in the driver's license office, a slip of paper bearing a printed number in one hand. She was going to have to wait longer than if she'd had an appointment, but the place wasn't as crowded as it could have been.

She'd already canceled her debit card and her only credit card. And she had a key to her apartment. Fortunately, the apartment manager liked her and sent the maintenance guy to the hardware store right away.

Paige glanced at the others waiting as she slipped into the back row. Reading would help pass the time. Unfortunately, she didn't have the Kindle app on the phone Tanner had given her. Maybe she could figure out how to download something.

She reached into her purse, then hesitated. The phone was still lying on her end table, connected to the charger. If Tanner tried to contact her and couldn't get a hold of her, he'd be worried.

When she'd hugged him in Jasper, she'd entertained fantasies of something less final than goodbye. She didn't expect professions of love. Or even talk of pursuing anything beyond friendship. She didn't expect it, but she'd hoped.

She should have known better. Tanner's past was every bit as rough as hers, but they'd gone in opposite directions. He'd joined the police academy and she'd joined a gang. He'd spent the last decade upholding the law, and she'd spent half of it in prison. She wasn't what noble, law-abiding men look for in a woman.

For the next hour, she tried unsuccessfully to steer her thoughts away from Tanner. When the clerk finally called her name, she heaved a sigh of relief.

Fifteen minutes later, she was headed out of the parking lot with a brand-new driver's license. She'd stop at Jake's for a short visit, then head home and text Tanner. Or maybe she'd call him. Because she really wanted to hear his voice.

She shook her head. She was pathetic.

After a series of turns, she drove along a sparsely wooded street in an older neighborhood. Finally, she pulled into a cracked concrete driveway and stopped behind an older Dodge Charger. The wood frame house was old but well kept. Jake's grandmother was in a nursing home nearby, but Jake took good care of her property.

Paige stepped from the car and walked between Jake's Charger and the newer model Blazer next to it. The Blazer belonged to Mark, Jake's older brother, also known as Mad Dog. Paige refused to call him anything except Mark.

Actually, she avoided contact with him whenever possible. He'd finished his last prison term three months ago. And Jake's life had been going downhill ever since.

As she stepped onto the porch, voices bled through

the front door, one of those court TV shows. She rang the bell, and the curtains to the right shifted. Moments later, the front door swung inward, and Jake stood in the opening, his eyebrows lifting, then drawing together in a mixture of surprise and hesitation. Most of the swelling in her face had gone down, but the bruising would be obvious for several more days.

She brought a hand to her cheek. "It's a long story. I would've called first, but I left my phone on the charger at home."

He looked past her to scan the driveway and front yard. Was he expecting someone else?

Finally, he backed up and motioned her inside. Mark lay on the couch, barefoot and shirtless. She'd never liked him. He was a dealer. The cops knew it, too. But they'd never gotten anything to stick except a couple of possession charges. Mark was too smart.

As she walked into the room, he made an attempt to sit up, then winced and lay back down. A huge gauze bandage wrapped his rib cage.

She raised her brows. "What happened to you?"

Before Mark could answer, Jake cut in. "He was walking to the store and got jumped by some guys. They shot him and left him for dead." He looked at her for several moments. "I could ask you the same thing."

"I got jumped, too. Some chicks weren't happy with my tattoo removal."

He slanted a glance at his brother, then returned his gaze to her. "Since Mad Dog here is hogging the couch, how about we go hang out in the cave?"

The "cave" was the basement, which, in spite of its nickname, was quite comfortable. With two overstuffed couches, a recliner, a big-screen TV and a fridge holding a variety of refreshments, it was a favorite hangout spot.

He held out a hand, and she led the way toward the closed door next to the kitchen. As she descended the stairs, a faint vinegary scent wrapped around her. She reached the bottom and rounded the corner. Several objects littered the coffee table—lighters, pieces of burned and discolored foil, white powder residue.

Jake waved a hand that direction. "You'll have to excuse my brother's *toys* over there. I'm still working on him."

Paige frowned. She'd chased the dragon enough times to know what she was looking at. And she wasn't gullible enough to believe that Jake had had no part in it.

She claimed a seat on the couch, and Jake sat on the front edge of the recliner. After crumpling the pieces of foil into a single ball, he brushed the residue onto the floor. Finally, he sat back and the footrest swung out. "Tell me about your trip."

"It didn't go like planned. My brother went with me." She gave him the abridged version, ending with Tommy being murdered and the killers coming after her. "I hit my head and ended up with total amnesia."

Jake studied her, eyes alert, as if trying to decipher something she wasn't telling him.

"I have my full memory now. But in the meantime, God sent someone to rescue me."

At the thought of Tanner, her stomach fluttered, and she silently scolded herself. She needed to quit thinking of him like that.

Easier said than done. The problem was, she cared for him a lot, not as her rescuer, but as a man. A beautiful, kind, considerate, brave and selfless man.

"You want something to drink? Coke? Sprite?"

"I'll take a Sprite."

He kicked in the footrest on the recliner and headed toward the fridge. An inked city skyline stretched across his upper back, visible over the top of his T-shirt.

"You got a new tattoo."

"I got it right before you left." He removed a Sprite and a beer from the fridge and placed them both on the counter.

She stared at the design. It was Atlanta. She recognized the silhouette of the Bank of America Plaza, rising to a sharp point. An odd premonition slid through her. Had something bad happened there? No, that was ridiculous. She'd never been to the building.

Jake popped the top off his beer, then laid the bottle opener on the counter before bringing her the Sprite. Once he'd settled himself in the recliner again, he took a long swig.

"So, these guys who shot your brother. You saw them do it?"

"Yeah. Then they came after me."

"Did you know them?"

"No. One held Tanner and me up at the storage unit here, and the other shot at us in Murphy. They're both behind bars now."

He released a long, slow breath. "So they've been caught."

"Yeah." But she couldn't shake the feeling that she was missing something important.

"Having amnesia must have been scary."

"It was." Without Tanner, it would have been downright terrifying.

"Did you forget about me?"

"I forgot about everybody. I didn't even know who *I* was. I didn't know my name, where I lived, where I worked."

"But your memory has returned? All of it?"

What was with all the questions? "Yes. I finally feel like there aren't any other holes."

"Good."

She stretched her legs out in front of her and crossed them at the ankles. "Did you do anything exciting while I was gone?"

He shrugged. "Just been hanging with Mad Dog. Got laid off."

"When?"

"A couple weeks ago. Work's been too slow."

Paige frowned. He was a good mechanic. Did he get laid off or fired? She nailed him with a stern gaze. "Be honest with me, Jake. Have you gone back to using?"

"No way." He took a couple more swigs of beer. "I gave that stuff up before I came to Atlanta. I'd be pretty stupid to go back to it."

Yeah, he would. Actually, they were both stupid to start it to begin with. "You wouldn't lie to me, would you?"

"You're one of my best friends. I'd never lie to you."

Yeah, he would. And she'd be hard-pressed to tell. He'd always been too good at it.

He tipped up the bottle and downed the last of his beer. When he went to retrieve another one, she stared at his back. That sense of uneasiness blanketed her again.

Something about that new tattoo bothered her. It wasn't the Bank of America Plaza, like she'd thought earlier. It was the whole tattoo. She suppressed a shudder.

What was wrong with her? It was a skyline. Nothing

could be more innocuous than a bunch of buildings. It wasn't like he had a skull and crossbones or the grim reaper tattooed on his back.

An image flashed through her mind, another inked design—one she found disturbing, not because of the tattoos themselves, but because the man sporting them killed her brother.

The image came into sharper focus. Two or three random geometric shapes. Or maybe they weren't random. Maybe they were part of a picture.

Like a city skyline.

Her sharp intake of air fell just short of a full-blown gasp. He turned toward her, refrigerator door still open.

"What?"

"Nothing." The single word sounded strained, as if something squeezed her airway.

He shut the door and studied her, dark eyes alert. It took all her effort to sit still and not run for the stairway.

"You remember, don't you?"

"Remember what?" The nonchalance she attempted fell flat. At one time, she could lie with ease. Not anymore. That was another area of her life God had changed.

He reached under his shirt and pulled out a small pistol. He'd probably slipped it into his waistband before answering the door.

She didn't even try to keep the alarm out of her voice. "What are you doing?"

"You remember." His tone was soft, his calmness mocking the panic ricocheting through her. "You saw the tattoo."

She glanced toward the steps, then frantically scanned

the small windows at the top of the back wall. Ever since
Tanner had come into her life, he'd protected her.

But he wasn't coming. She'd sent him home. Another
bad choice. Her life had been marked by bad choices.

Jake moved closer, then stopped well out of her reach.
"I never intended for you to get hurt. But I couldn't let
Torpedo get away with what he did."

Paige bristled at the use of Tommy's street name.
Since leaving Orlando, she'd refused to call him by anything but the nickname he'd had all his life.

"He didn't just steal from me. He almost got Mad
Dog killed."

Paige gave a slow nod. Mark wasn't jumped walking to the store. He got shot during the drug deal that
went bad.

Jake shook his head. "A few days before that, my
brother had a feeling Torpedo was gonna try to rip us
off. Since you'd loaned him your car, Mad Dog put the
tracking device on it."

"And you followed it and killed my friend."

"We had no idea Torpedo was with you. At least not
then." The look he shot her was accusatory. "You told
me you were going alone."

"I was. Tommy called me at the last minute and
asked to go with me."

He nodded. "After we found out where you guys had
gone, Bruno dropped Ace and me off. We took care of
Torpedo, and Bruno picked us up near the Nantahala
Outdoor Center."

Bruno, Ace and Jake. The first two were in jail. But
there was a third. She'd made a huge mistake.

She rose and took a step toward him. "I won't say
anything. Just let me go." She took another step. "When

I first got to Atlanta, you promised me you wouldn't rat me out to my gang and you've kept that promise. Your secret is safe with me, too." Another step. If she could get close enough to kick the gun out of his hand, she might be able to escape.

"Stop!" The sharp tone brought her up short. "I won't go back to jail. I don't want to do this, but I've got to."

"If you don't want to do it, don't."

"I have no choice. I like you. But I like my freedom more."

Hopelessness descended on her. She believed him. He really didn't want to kill her.

But what difference did it make?

No matter how she sugarcoated it, *reluctantly killed* was still *dead*.

Tanner turned down yet another Atlanta street, despair bearing down on him. He was on the outer edge of his search perimeter and had found only two red Ford Focuses. Both were newer models than the one Paige drove.

He'd even given Millie a call and asked if she knew Jake. She'd said she'd met him and knew he was Paige's friend, but didn't know where he lived.

Tanner braked at a red light and slammed his hand down on the steering wheel. There was little he hated more than feeling helpless. From lying powerless while his sister died, to being weak and defenseless in the foster homes he'd landed in, to being unable to prevent the inevitable in the lives of the people on his beat, he'd experienced it too many times.

Now Paige needed him. And he once again found himself helpless. Whatever it took, he had to find her.

With nothing more than a gut feeling and some un-answered texts and phone calls, he didn't have enough to file a missing persons report. Since he'd just commu-nicated with her less than three hours ago, Atlanta PD wouldn't take him seriously. He wouldn't blame them.

The light changed, and he stepped on the gas. When he turned down a side street, his pulse picked up speed. It was an older neighborhood. Narrow porches jutted out from small houses on postage stamp–sized lots.

He scanned the driveways, as he'd been doing for the last half hour. Ahead, the rear end of a small red car poked out from behind an SUV in the next drive-way. He stepped on the gas, his heart pounding out an erratic rhythm.

As he approached the property line, the car came fully into view. Definitely an older model. It had to be Paige's. The location of the dents even seemed to match.

He pulled into the driveway and stopped next to her car. Two other vehicles were there, parked in front, a Charger and a Blazer. Paige had said Jake lived with his brother. Apparently they were both home.

When he stepped from his truck, a faint masculine voice reached him. It was a low hum, without much in-flection. Not angry or threatening. Maybe the three of them were sitting inside, just talking.

So why wasn't she responding to his texts or calls? Her phone wasn't dead. When he spoke with her, she was charging it.

He closed his truck door and moved toward the house. The voices grew louder. He stepped onto the porch and frowned. What he heard wasn't conversa-tion; it was the TV.

He rang the bell and waited, hand resting near the

pistol holstered at his hip. He rang it again. Heavy drapes covered the windows on each side of the door. Curtains and miniblinds covered the other windows, too.

After ringing the bell a third time, a gruff voice called from within.

"Who is it?"

"Tanner Brody. I'm a friend of Paige's."

"She's not here."

Tanner frowned. If her car was there, along with both Jake's and his brother's, Paige was there. Those guys didn't seem like the type to afford multiple vehicles.

"Do you know where she went?"

"She's with Jake."

"Jake's car is still here." He might as well test the one-car theory.

"Maybe they walked."

Tanner's jaw tightened. What now? A request to come inside would be pointless. And if he kicked in the door, he'd be arrested or shot.

He walked toward the Silverado, mind spinning. In a situation like this, Paige would pray. And coming from Paige, God would listen. Tanner couldn't expect the same response.

When he got to the truck, he pulled out his phone and dialed 911. He'd get the police to come out and check. They'd enter forcibly if necessary. If he was wrong, he'd deal with it later.

When the dispatcher came on, Tanner explained how Paige had already had several attempts on her life and he believed she was still in danger.

"I'm standing outside a house now." He gave the dispatcher the address. "Her car's here, and I believe she's inside." And he wasn't sure he should wait for the police to arrive.

He cranked the truck and backed up from the drive. An abandoned house was three doors down. He'd passed it on the way to Jake's.

By the time he finished the call, he'd already parked and was jogging through backyards. He didn't have a game plan beyond learning what he could and following his gut.

When he got to Jake's yard, he stood half-hidden by a tree. Wide, squat windows ran along the bottom of the house, all covered in black plastic except the one at the end. Basement windows. If Paige was being held against her will, that was likely where she'd be.

He jogged toward the house, then crept across the back, crouched low. When he reached the uncovered window, he dropped to his hands and knees. Its frame was warped, the bottom corner an inch shy of closing.

He leaned forward, then drew back. That brief glimpse was enough to take in a heating unit in the corner, a stack of plastic bins and some open wooden shelves. The area seemed to be used for storage, separate from the rest of the basement.

The TV still played, barely audible from the back of the house. A masculine voice came from nearby, but it was too faint to make out the words. He leaned forward again, and another voice reached him, female this time.

"Do you really want to do this?"

The voice was Paige's, and he didn't like the sound of the question.

"No, I don't want to do this." There was agitation and tension in the tone. "But I refuse to spend my life in prison."

Tanner glanced around, panic spiraling through him. Sirens sounded in the distance.

God, please let them be for Paige. Maybe God wouldn't listen to him. But it was worth a shot.

The sirens seemed to be moving closer. But the units were still another two or three minutes out. Judging from the conversation he'd heard, Paige might not have that long.

He jumped up and ran toward the back door. At least two men were in the house, one in the basement with Paige and the other in the front room. He drew his weapon and tried the knob. Locked. There wouldn't be any stealth.

He brought his right leg up, then thrust outward. His foot connected next to the lock. The jamb splintered and the door swung inward.

A kitchen was in front of him, an open doorway straight ahead, leading into a living room. He charged inside, pistol raised. To the right was a closed door, probably to the basement. A grunt came from the living room, as if someone was struggling to get up.

Tanner reached the door in three large strides and swung it open, eyes still on the living room. A head, shoulder and one arm appeared around the corner, and a shot rang out. Tanner returned fire as he slipped behind the door.

Commotion erupted in the basement—thuds, grunts, the sounds of fists against flesh. Was that how the man planned to kill Paige, by beating her to death?

He ran down the stairs, taking them two at a time. When he got to the bottom, another crack rent the air, sending a white-hot poker through the back of his thigh.

His knee buckled as he spun to get off his own shot, and he fell into the railing.

The sirens stopped abruptly. The man above disappeared, and heavy footsteps sounded across the wooden floor.

Tanner limped around the corner. A man slugged Paige in the side of the head, knocking her to the floor, then dived for the pistol lying a few feet away. Tanner leveled his weapon. Moisture ran down his leg, soaking his jeans. "Put it down, Jake."

The other man's gaze shifted to him. Indecision flashed in his eyes.

"Give it up. The cops are right outside."

A knock sounded above. "Police. We're coming in!"

Then there were multiple sets of footsteps. Other officers had apparently entered through the back.

Tanner leaned against the wall separating the stairs from the rest of the room. His pistol was still aimed at Jake, whose weapon was trained on Paige. From knee to hip, his left leg was on fire. Strength poured from his limbs with every beat of his heart.

Someone descended the stairs behind him. It had to be one of the cops. Jake's brother would be long gone.

He cast a glance at Paige. She'd made it onto her hands and knees. Her lip was bleeding, and one eye was already starting to swell.

An officer rounded the corner. For several moments longer, Jake maintained his stance.

"Drop the weapons." The command was sharp.

Tanner cast the officer a sideways glance. The order was for him, too. But as long as Jake had his pistol pointed at Paige, Tanner wasn't moving.

"I'm the one who called it in. I'm a cop."

More footsteps sounded on the steps, and a second officer stepped around the corner. Jake lowered his weapon. Tanner's own dropped to his side, his arm too weak to hold it up. As he watched handcuffs snap around Jake's wrists, darkness encroached on the edges of his vision.

Paige straightened and stumbled toward him, her face framed with a shadowed circle that was growing smaller by the second. Her arms slid around his neck.

"You came. I needed you and you were there." The ringing in his ears grew louder, her words more distant, as if she were falling down a well. Or maybe he was the one falling.

Her face swam in front of him, then started to fade. Darkness descended over everything. His eyes drifted shut.

Soft lips pressed against his own.

His weapon clattered to the floor.

And his world went silent.

ELEVEN

Paige pushed a wheelchair down the wide hall, tennis shoes almost silent against the vinyl floor. Doors lined the walls on either side, some open, some closed. Their positions weren't important. She wasn't looking into any of the rooms.

She hated hospitals.

None of her visits had been pleasant. And she'd had many. Tanner twisted his head around to look up at her. "You should've been checked, too."

"I'm fine, aside from a few bruises and a busted lip." She'd already been hospitalized once that month and would rather skip the repeat. Of course, during the Bryson City stay, she'd been too confused to realize how badly she hated hospitals.

She stopped in front of the elevators, and Tanner reached for the down button. A set of crutches lay at an angle across his lap, and he'd kept his weight shifted to his right hip the entire ride.

When she'd seen him step around the corner at Jake's, she thought she was hallucinating. She'd had no idea how he knew to come. She still didn't. But he'd saved her life, and for that she was grateful. She didn't realize he'd been hurt until she'd kissed him and he'd slid down the wall unconscious.

Heat crept up her cheeks. What had she been thinking? He hadn't mentioned it, so maybe he'd already been checking out and wasn't aware of what she'd done.

Tanner shifted, then ended up in the same position, weight toward his right hip. "Tell me how I'm getting home again."

"I'm driving you in your truck. Then Colton's bringing me back to Atlanta." She'd explained it last night, after he'd come out of surgery, but he'd still been pretty out of it.

"I'm not sure I like that arrangement." He grinned up at her. "Don't believe a thing he says about me."

"I might get some juicy tidbits? Sounds interesting." The doors opened, and she pushed him into the elevator. "I took your keys when I left last night and brought your truck to the parking garage. Then someone from the mission took me to my car. Jake's neighborhood's not as bad as my old one, but I didn't want to risk you coming back to your truck on blocks and the wheels missing."

"Thanks."

When she pulled away from the hospital a short time later, Tanner was leaning against the door, face pinched with pain. Guilt surged through her. It was *her* brother who got them into this mess and her friend who decided she needed to die. And now Tanner had taken a bullet.

She eased to a stop at a traffic light and looked over at him. "Why did you come back?" He hadn't been coherent enough to question him last night, and she'd worked at Millie's Place from six this morning until an hour and a half ago. "How'd you know I was in trouble?"

"I had a gut feeling. What really did it, though, was remembering what you said about Jake spending time with your brother. The more I thought about it, the more I wondered if he was involved in the same business that had gotten Thomas killed. When I couldn't get hold of you, I couldn't shake the feeling something was wrong."

"I'd forgotten to take my phone off the charger. It wasn't until I got home last night that I saw the texts and missed calls." Realization slammed into her. "If I would've had my phone, I'd have assured you everything was fine. By the time you'd have realized I was in trouble, it would've been too late. Forgetting my phone saved my life." She smiled. "Sometimes God takes our mess-ups and turns them into something good."

"That's a pretty extreme example."

"It is." She flipped on her signal and crept up the 75 North ramp. After she'd eased into traffic, she rested her head against the seat. She might as well get comfortable. At a quarter till five, they weren't going anywhere fast.

She released a sigh. It was finally over. Everyone associated with her brother's murder had been apprehended. And she'd come out of the whole thing relatively unscathed.

Physically anyway.

Mentally and emotionally, she wasn't so sure. Another person close to her had betrayed her. She hadn't fully let down her guard with Jake, but she'd allowed him to get closer than she had anyone else in a long time.

Tanner had accused her of building walls. He was

right. And she didn't see them coming down anytime soon. In fact, wrapping herself in a cocoon and never coming out sounded like a good option at the moment.

Tanner shifted next to her. "Thanks for driving me home."

"It's the least I could do, seeing as you saved my life and all."

"It was nothing. I'm just glad it's over."

"No more bad guys out there?"

He lifted one brow. "There'll always be bad guys. But I think we got the ones who were after you."

"Is that what your gut tells you?"

A slow smile spread across his face. "Yep."

"Listening to your gut, you do that a lot."

"It makes me good at what I do."

She nodded. Having that natural instinct would be important in police work. But Tanner had so much more. "That's not all that makes you good. In the short time I've known you, I've seen a lot that impresses me. Your dedication. Your compassion. Your determination to protect the innocent. Murphy is blessed to have you." She gasped. "You're supposed to start your new job next week. Is getting hurt putting that in jeopardy?"

"I called them today from the hospital. They're holding the job."

She heaved a sigh of relief. With everything she'd put him through, if she were the cause of him losing his job, she'd never forgive herself.

Over the next forty-five minutes, traffic gradually lightened. They grabbed a bite to eat in Ellijay, her treat this time. It was good to feel independent again.

When she stopped at the last traffic light in Blue Ridge, she glanced over at Tanner. His head was leaning against the window, and both eyes were closed. In another fifteen or twenty minutes, she'd have him home. In the meantime, she'd let him sleep. The doctors probably had him on some pretty hefty pain meds. He'd likely had a restless night, too.

She was just turning onto 294 when Tanner lifted his head. "Sorry. I fell asleep."

"No need to apologize. Is there anything I can do for you before I head home? You'll be a little incapacitated for a few days."

"No, I'm good. Fortunately, I got the lawn mowed yesterday. Do you need me to call Colton?"

"I can do it." At his raised brows, she continued, "You gave me his number last night."

He invited her inside, then opened the vertical blinds so they could watch for Colton. Five minutes later, a gold Highlander pulled into the drive.

They rose from the couch, and she stepped forward to give Tanner a hug, careful not to throw him off balance. He had a crutch under each arm, his right leg carrying most of his weight.

She ended the hug with two pats on the back. "Take care of yourself."

"You, too. Try to stay away from guys with guns."

"Like you?"

He grinned. "*Bad* guys with guns."

"I'll keep that in mind." Why did this goodbye feel so much more permanent?

Because he was ready to move on. She and her problems had consumed his life long enough. He was putting everything behind him, and she needed to do the same.

She walked out the door and climbed into the Highlander's passenger seat. As Colton backed from the drive, she waved at Tanner through the front wind-shield. He was standing on the porch, watching them go.

A vise clamped down on her chest. What if she never saw him again?

She squared her shoulders and shored up her defenses. This was what she was good at, walling off her emotions, shutting people out. She'd been doing it all her life.

Except Tanner wasn't like the others. He'd come back for her, even when she'd told him not to. He wouldn't betray anyone. He always put others' needs above his own. For that woman blessed enough to find forever with him, he'd always be there. Through thick and thin.

But that wouldn't be her. Her life was too messed up, her past too tainted. The same way that crown on her arm would never completely disappear, even after her last laser treatment, all her bad deeds cast a permanent shadow over her soul.

God had forgiven her. But how could she expect Tanner to look past the woman she used to be when she'd never been able to forgive herself?

Tanner stood gripping the chair in front of him, the padded top of a crutch tucked under each arm. Voices swelled all around him. Half a dozen musicians and singers were spread across the platform, and song lyrics were displayed on a screen over the drummer's head.

His first time inside a church during his adult life, he'd have preferred an aisle seat in the back row. But that apparently wasn't how Colton and Mandy did church. They'd walked inside and marched almost to the front, greeting people along the way and introducing him to their friends. Now, in the third row, hemmed in between Colton and some guy every bit of six foot five, Tanner couldn't escape if he wanted to.

The past three Sundays, Colton had invited him, but he'd declined. He'd had a good excuse. Sitting for extended periods, even on padded chairs, had been miserable. But now, more than three weeks postinjury, the pain in his leg had lessened to tenderness. So here he was, in church for the first time in well over a decade.

But it wasn't that bad. The band was good, the atmosphere laid-back. Not like the starchy environment he remembered, where he'd been scared to death he was going to say or do something wrong.

When the song service ended, the singers and musicians exited the platform. Tanner leaned his crutches against the chair in front of him and took a seat with everyone else. A man in the front row climbed the three steps onto the stage, with the use of his own crutches. One pants leg was cut off at the knee and hemmed shut. This wasn't the pastor. Colton had said they were having a guest speaker.

The man took a seat on a stool and stood his crutches against the wooden lectern. Though he wore a polo shirt and Dockers, with his buzz cut and muscular build, it was easy to imagine him in camo.

The picture wasn't far off. He'd done three tours in Afghanistan. Well, two and a half. The third was cut short when he stepped on an IED.

He went on to explain how God had been with him, even when he didn't know it, during a childhood as dysfunctional as Tanner's, through all the years he ran from Him, even through the years he hated Him. By the time he lost his leg, he'd been in more need of emotional than physical healing.

Tanner could relate. Opening up to Paige had been cathartic, but the memories hurt as much as they ever had.

As the speaker relayed his experiences, the message tugged at Tanner. The man wasn't using his religion to manipulate others. Instead, he seemed to have a genuine relationship with God and wanted to share it with everyone around him. Actually, so did Colton and Mandy. And so did Paige.

"Through it all, God never abandoned me." The ex-soldier's words drew Tanner back. "Looking over my life, I can see His hand in all my circumstances."

Tanner frowned. God couldn't have been in the events of his childhood—witnessing his sister's murder, being bounced from one foster home to the next, landing in a group home.

But maybe God *had* been there the night his sister was killed. He should have died with her. Instead, his life was spared.

What about the group home? Was it coincidence that he and Colton landed there together, or did God orchestrate that, knowing it would be what Tanner needed? How many other blessings would he find if he really looked?

Instead of abandoning him, had God really been with him the entire time?

When he walked out of church sometime later, the same questions still circled through his mind. He didn't have any answers yet. But something nagged at him, the suspicion that all the years he'd blamed God for turning His back, he'd been wrong.

He climbed into the Highlander and forty minutes later was seated around the table with Colton and

Mandy, a pot roast and other fixings in the center. Liam looked on from his high chair. The invitation to church and the invitation to lunch had come at the same time. Actually, it had been a dual invitation every time Colton issued it.

After blessing the food, Colton started the serving bowls around the table. "Have you seen Paige?"

"We've talked on the phone a few times."

"Is that all? I figured you guys would have gotten together before now."

"It's only been three weeks." He shrugged. "She's busy with her job and her volunteer work with the mission." And he totally missed her.

And Colton knew it. Tanner could see it in his eyes. But Colton didn't bring up Paige's name again until they were alone in the living room, Mandy having gone to put Liam down for a nap.

"Paige and I had a good talk on the way to Atlanta."

Oh, no. Just what he'd been afraid of. He narrowed his eyes at his friend. "What did you tell her?"

"How do you feel about her?"

"We're friends."

"You didn't answer my question."

Tanner crossed his arms. "You didn't answer mine, either."

"How do you feel about her?"

Tanner sighed. He had a stubborn streak, but once Colton latched onto something, he didn't let go. "I like her. A lot."

"Are you in love with her?"

He slanted a glance at his friend. It was a question he'd asked himself. One he'd dismissed before digging deeply enough to get an answer. "How I feel doesn't matter."

"Since when?"

He whirled on Colton. "You know my history." He didn't try to keep the frustration from his tone. "With all Paige has been through, do you really think she deserves someone like me? I wouldn't wish that on my worst enemy."

"Actually, I *do* think Paige deserves someone like you. *She's* the one who thinks she doesn't deserve you."

"See, I told you."

"She thinks she's not good enough."

Colton's words were like a kick to the gut. "You know that's not true. Did you set her straight?"

"Not my place, bro. I can't speak for you."

Tanner glared at him. Colton knew him well enough to speak for him and had no qualms about doing so when it suited him. "Fine. I'll call her and let her know that's not the case. But it's not going to make a difference. I'm not serious relationship material. Why do you think Brittney dumped me for Kevin?"

"Because she's too messed up to know what she wants. The same reason she dumped Kevin for another guy in the department."

"Huh?"

"Found out on Facebook. I never got around to unfriending him." He shrugged. "You managed to hang on to her longer than Kevin did. That should count for something. But this conversation isn't about them. It's about you and Paige."

Yeah, the conversation was about him and Paige, but his brain was stuck on Kevin. Brittney had dumped him, too. He should feel like doing a fist pump with a "Take that!"

But he knew how rotten the guy felt and didn't have it in him to gloat. Not that he planned to call and offer sympathy. It would take more than sitting through one church service for a move like that.

Mandy swept back into the room and approached them. "Now that I've got Liam down, I'm going to steal a nap, too." She lifted a hand in farewell. "It was great having you join us, Tanner. I hope we'll make this a regular Sunday event. Church *and* lunch."

Oh, yeah. Mandy's cooking would be great consolation for spending Sunday mornings in church. Although the bribe was no longer necessary.

Colton took her hand. "Go get some rest. I'll do the dishes."

"You're the best." She leaned forward and kissed him.

Tanner beat down a twinge of envy. His friends' relationship—the respect and camaraderie, the love-filled glances, the sense they'd found their soul mates—it all shone a spotlight on everything that was out of reach for him.

Or was it? Maybe he'd tried to find it with the wrong women. But was there a *right* woman? Could he find with Paige what Colton had found with Mandy? More importantly, could Paige find it with him?

Colton watched his wife walk down the hall, then returned his attention to Tanner. "So, what are you going to do?"

"I don't know." He didn't have to ask Colton what he meant. "I've got to think about it." Paige would pray about it. Not a bad idea.

"What's your gut telling you right now?"

Tanner pursed his lips. His gut was telling him that even though Paige was out of danger, she needed him. And he needed her. That instead of their pasts making a future together impossible, maybe their shared traumas would make their bond even stronger.

He looked at Colton, his gaze steady. "That I've found something special, and I'd be nuts if I walked away."

A smile spread across Colton's face. "I couldn't have said it better myself."

Six eager faces turned toward Paige as she approached a table that sat six inches lower than the others in the room. The mission followed its four o'clock Sunday church service with dinner. And her kids always insisted on sitting with her instead of their parents.

As she laid her plate and drink on the table, one of the children jumped up and wrapped both arms around her legs. "I love you, Miss Paige."

Paige bent down to hug her and kiss the top of her head. Her hair was stringy, and the tattered T-shirt looked about two sizes too big.

And Paige loved her. She loved them all. How could she have forgotten these little ones?

"I love you, too, Megan." She eased into the chair on the end, not intended for grown-ups any more than the table was. Paper plates sat in front of all of them, holding varied amounts of chicken, mashed potatoes and green beans.

"Brian called me ugly at school." The complaint came from the little girl adjacent to her.

"When?"

"A few days ago."

Paige tucked the child's hair behind her ear, then cupped her face. "You're not ugly, Keira. You're beautiful. And you know what else? God is the king, and you're His child. So, guess what that makes you."

"What?"

"A princess."

The girl's eyes widened, and a smile spread across her face.

Justin, two chairs down, waved excitedly. "I got a B on my math test."

Pride swelled inside for this at-risk little boy who'd fallen so far behind he'd had little chance of catching up. Since Christmas, she'd tutored him right after work three times a week. It was paying off.

She leaned over the table, hand held up for a high five. "I knew you could do it. You're going to ace the third grade."

Justin stood to slap her palm. All the pride she felt was reflected in his big brown eyes.

As she picked up her fork, her gaze slid over to a figure standing against the wall ten or twelve feet away, a crutch tucked under each arm. Her hand froze midway to her plate, and she did a double take.

"Tanner?"

He pushed himself away from the wall and approached. The smile he gave her had a warmth and softness that made her stomach do somersaults.

"How long have you been standing there?"

"A few minutes."

She'd been so focused on helping the kids and getting her own food, she hadn't seen him come in.

"What are you doing here?"

"I came to see you."

Yeah, she figured that. What she wanted to know was why he decided to drive over instead of calling.

"How about joining us for dinner?" She slid her chair to the side to make room. "We'll even let you sit in a grown-up chair."

He put a hand over his stomach and moaned. "I'm still full from lunch. Colton and Mandy invited me over. After church."

Her pulse kicked up. "You went with them?"

"I did."

"How was it?"

"Different. In a good way."

"Does that mean there might be more services in your future?"

"It does. Especially if Mandy feeds me."

He gave her a goofy grin, and she slapped him on the arm. After he sat in a chair she'd swiped from a nearby table, she put a hand on his shoulder. "Kids, this is Mr. Tanner. He's a policeman."

Tanner said hi and received a chorus of greetings.

"How come you have crutches?" Justin eyed the pair leaning against the table. "Did you get shot?"

Tanner laughed. "As a matter of fact, I did."

"By a bad guy?" Awe had seeped into his tone.

"Yep. A bad guy who's now in jail." They'd gotten the news that same evening—authorities had apprehended Mark when he'd tried to slip back into the house.

Keira looked at Paige, eyes round. "Is Mr. Tanner your boyfriend?"

Heat crept up her cheeks, and she gave an uneasy laugh. "No, he's—"

"If she'll let me be."

She swiveled her head toward Tanner. Her heart took flight, and her stomach followed. This time it wasn't just somersaults. There were a couple of backflips thrown in. She opened her mouth to respond, but her brain had disengaged.

Tanner filled the gap. "When you're finished here, I'd like to talk. We have a misunderstanding to clear up."

By the time the plates were empty, Tanner had gotten well acquainted with the kids. He did great with them, even teased the two boys. Judging from his interactions with her kids, he'd probably been well liked as a beat cop.

Or not. Kids might have a hard time believing he was the good guy if they associated the uniform with Daddy being hauled to jail.

After the kids had dispersed, Tanner and Paige rose from the table.

"Follow me to my place and we can go for a walk." Paige eyed his crutches. "Or maybe a walk isn't a good idea."

"I can make it. I've gotten pretty good at maneuvering on these things."

She nodded. "Stanton Park isn't far from where I live."

When they arrived at her apartment complex, night was still an hour away. Since moving to the Peoplestown area, she'd felt relatively safe. It wasn't middle-class suburbia, but it was leaps ahead of her last place.

She headed toward the sidewalk, and Tanner fell into step beside her. For several moments, she listened to the *click* of the crutches while she waited for him to speak. Whatever he had to say, it warranted a drive to Atlanta instead of a phone call. All through dinner, she'd almost gone crazy wondering what it was.

When the moments stretched into a minute, she looked up at him. He stared straight ahead, brow furrowed, lips pressed together.

This was a side of Tanner she hadn't seen before. He always seemed decisive and confident, even with men shooting at them. Now he acted unsure, as if he didn't know his next step.

"You wanted to talk to me about something?"

"Yeah. I'm just not sure where to start." He drew in a deep breath. "I've missed you. I figured once this was over, we'd return to our lives and that would be that." He fell silent.

"And?"

"It hasn't worked out that way. You've been on my mind. A lot. Then Colton, meddling friend that he is, said some things that got me thinking."

Yeah, Colton had talked to her, too. He'd been convinced Tanner felt more than friendship for her. She'd set him straight right away.

Tanner halted. She drew to a stop next to him and waited for him to continue.

"There's so much in you that I admire. Your strength and resilience. Your concern for others. Your faith. We share the same interests. We come from the same rotten background. We understand each other. I think we'd be making a big mistake if we walked away without at least exploring the possibilities."

She stared up at him, trying to sort out the jumble of emotions coiled inside. Tanner seemed like the embodiment of every fantasy she'd ever had. Which meant he was too good to be true. If she let down her guard, she'd open herself up to more hurt when he moved on.

"Why?" She resumed walking again. "Why are you considering a relationship now? I'm still the same woman I was before—former gang member, convicted felon—"

"That was never an issue with me."

She flung her arms wide. "My past affiliations almost got you killed."

"Those were your brother's affiliations, not yours."

"Jake was mine."

"He was a threat only because of his connection with your brother."

They reached the end of the road and turned toward the park.

He continued, "You were right. I wasn't willing to consider anything beyond friendship. But that had nothing to do with you. I didn't believe I had anything to offer." He kicked at a soda can someone had tossed and sent it clattering down the sidewalk. "I've told you about my past. I have no clue what goes into building a stable relationship. With everything you'd overcome, I felt you deserved so much better."

She blinked and shook her head. *He* thought *she* deserved better? He couldn't be serious. "I'm the one with the sketchy past."

"Your past doesn't have to shape your future. That fact was driven home to me this afternoon, watching you with the children."

She raised her brows. "How?"

"All those kids were clamoring for your attention. But you made each one feel special. I kept asking myself where you learned that. It wasn't because you'd been on the receiving end of that kind of love as a kid. From what you've told me, you didn't even have your physical needs met. Forget the emotional ones. But there you were, building up each of those kids, loving them like they're your own."

Her heart swelled with the admiration in his eyes, and warmth flowed through her. A long walkway stretched ahead of them, covered by the solar panels that made Stanton Atlanta's first energy-neutral park. It had been a regular part of her jogging route since she moved.

She gave him a rueful smile. "Loving kids is easy. They're pure and innocent and have no ulterior motives."

"It's more than that. Watching you, I realized you're going to be an amazing mother, even though you didn't have one yourself."

She nodded. "When I was eight years old, I made a vow that if I ever grew up and had children, I would be the mother I wished I'd had."

They emerged from under the covered walk, then followed the curved path around the splash pad at the center of the park. It wouldn't open until next week. As temperatures got warmer, the space would likely be filled with kids shooting each other with the water cannons and running through the streams spurting up from the ground.

He continued, attention focused straight ahead, "Positive role models give us a great foundation on which to build our lives, but negative ones can be a foundation, too, by giving us examples of the behaviors we *don't* want to emulate."

He released a sigh. "I didn't learn how to treat a

woman by watching a good father shower praise and kisses on my mother. I learned how *not* to treat a woman by watching my mother's men shout obscenities and slap her around."

He stopped and stared out over the ball field. "Neither of us has an example of how to build a solid relationship and a stable home. But there's something that we *do* have. Examples of what *not* to do." Sympathy filled his eyes. "I know you have some trust issues."

"That's an understatement." She heaved a sigh. "A lifetime of conditioning has taught me that anyone I allow close to me is going to eventually let me down. The last serious relationship I had was a year before I went to prison. Ever since, I've ended it before anything too serious could develop."

And what good had it done her? She'd avoided being hurt by a boyfriend but been set up by her brother and betrayed by her best friend.

He turned her to face him and took her hands in his, still balancing on his crutches. "You've had a lot of people turn on you. You have good reason to be cautious. But I'm asking you to let down your guard with me, like you did at Chevelle's and in your room afterward. I felt like I was seeing the real Paige, no barriers, and I liked what I saw."

The wall around her heart wobbled, threatening to collapse. She gave him a quivery smile. "I'll try."

"I'm not expecting changes overnight. All I'm asking is that you give me the opportunity to prove that I'm different from the guys who've taken advantage of you."

"I think you already have."

He released one hand to cup her cheek. "I don't have a good track record. My relationships always seem to end badly. But I've never betrayed someone, and I've never intentionally hurt anyone. If you'll trust me, I'll do everything in my power to prove to you that your trust isn't misplaced."

She swallowed hard, her heart pounding. What he was asking for was a commitment, and she wasn't there yet. But Tanner was right. She couldn't let her past determine her future.

"If you're trying so hard to earn my trust, the least I can do is try to give it."

Relief filled his eyes, and his lips lifted in a warm smile. His hand slid back to tangle in her hair, and he drew her closer. He was going to kiss her. And she wasn't sure she was ready for that, either.

She gave him a teasing smile. "So, if I understand what you told Keira correctly, you want to be my boyfriend."

"That's a start. But I'm thinking something much more long-term."

Warmth infused her chest again, then spread outward, all the way into her fingers and toes. Her heart pounded in an odd mix of excitement and trepidation.

"But you're in Murphy and I'm in Atlanta."

"Two hours apart. I know people whose daily commute is almost that long." He squeezed the hand he still held. "I love you, Paige, and I'm not letting you go. If that means selling my house and moving to Atlanta, so be it."

Her heart swelled. Tanner loved her, in spite of her past. And she loved him. She could no longer deny it. "Maybe I'd rather move to Murphy."

"That would work, too."

"I'd miss my kids."

"We have some of those." He grinned. "And there

are quite a few organizations that would love to have you volunteer."

She nodded. Since she'd signed a seven-month lease in February, she had another five months to pray about where God wanted her.

"Any other objections?"

Her thoughts still spun. In spite of how messed up they were, maybe they *did* have a foundation on which to build a future. Maybe together they could work to build the home they both wished they'd had.

But she'd have to let down her guard. Completely.

Sure, there was risk. Anything worthwhile involved risk. But she could lessen it by choosing wisely. It didn't take a sign from heaven to know that giving her heart to Tanner was the wisest choice she could make.

She'd no longer let her past define her future. Starting now, she was going to step out in faith. She'd trust God, and Tanner, with her heart.

She tilted her face upward and looked into warm green eyes. "No other objections."

"So, does that mean you'll marry me?"

"Are you asking?"

"I am. It can be a long engagement. But I'm making sure you don't get away."

"Why would I even try?"

He tilted his head and lifted a brow. "Is that a yes?"

"Yes." She pulled her hand from his to wrap both arms around his neck. "But I have a confession to make. I've been fighting feelings for you since the day you led me out of the woods."

"That's a long time to hold on to a secret like that." He gave her a teasing smile. "Any other confessions?"

"I think I fell in love with you when you insisted I take your thirty dollars."

"Any others?"

"One more. I'd really like for you to kiss me now."

The smile faded and all teasing left his eyes. His lips met hers, gently encouraging her to let down her guard and trust him.

She returned the kiss. He was everything she could ever want in a man.

All along, she'd known God had put Tanner in her path. She'd thought it was just to save her life.

Now she knew the truth.

It was also to heal her heart.

And maybe, in the process, she'd help heal his.

* * * * *

If you enjoyed this exciting story of suspense and intrigue, pick up these other stories from Carol J. Post:

SHATTERED HAVEN
HIDDEN IDENTITY
MISTLETOE JUSTICE
BURIED MEMORIES
REUNITED BY DANGER

Available now from Love Inspired Suspense!

Find more great reads at www.LoveInspired.com.

Dear Reader,

I hope you've enjoyed reading Paige and Tanner's story. This is the first book in a new series set in Murphy, North Carolina. I love the area, and it's been fun moving to a new setting.

Paige and Tanner both had very dysfunctional pasts. Paige's path to healing began when she heard about Christ's love from an unlikely source. But she still had to learn to view herself the way God sees her, as cherished and forgiven.

Tanner's only exposure to Christianity was through rules-oriented religion, and he believed he could never measure up. My church has a new mission statement, one that is very simple and to the point—Love God, Love Others. God demands holiness, but that message apart from love and forgiveness paints an incomplete picture of what the gospel is all about.

I hope you will be on the lookout for the second book in this series, where Bryce reconnects with his first love and they both find their happily-ever-after.

Love in Christ,
Carol J. Post

COMING NEXT MONTH FROM
Love Inspired® Suspense

Available July 3, 2018

STANDING FAST
Military K-9 Unit • by Maggie K. Black

When Chase McLear is accused of aiding a serial killer, the only person who believes he's innocent is his daughter's teacher, Maisy Lockwood... whose father was one of the killer's victims. Can Chase and his K-9 beagle prove his innocence so he can build a family with Maisy?

GONE
FBI: Special Crimes Unit • by Shirlee McCoy

FBI agent Sam Sheridan's mission is to take down a human trafficking ring and save missing teens—until he blows his cover to rescue a kidnapped woman. Ella McIntire came too close to a dangerous secret, and only Sam can protect her from the men determined to silence her.

COWBOY BODYGUARD
Gold Country Cowboys • by Dana Mentink

ER doctor Shannon Livingston defies a biker gang to save one of her patients and must turn to her secret husband to keep the woman's baby safe. She left Jack Thorn behind years ago, but will posing as the baby's parents reunite their hearts?

NO PLACE TO HIDE
by Lisa Harris

Former navy diver Ryan Kendall's father sent him to Brazil with a simple assignment: extract compromised witness Ellie Webb. But with Ellie determined to follow a lead on her father's murder into the Amazon, Ryan must protect her. As pirates chase them, though, can they survive the dangerous jungle?

STANDOFF AT MIDNIGHT MOUNTAIN
by Mary Alford

After her CIA operative brother disappears, leaving behind only a cryptic message, armed men target former agent Rachel Simmons for information. Pursued through the wilderness by highly trained—and very familiar—men, can Rachel and her ex, Agent Alex Booth, expose a conspiracy that goes deeper than they ever imagined?

ALASKAN HIDEOUT
by Sarah Varland

Emma Bass thought nothing could bring her to Alaska...or back to Tyler Dawson, who doesn't know he's the father of her child. But when danger chases her from home, she's desperate enough to run to Tyler— and hope he's forgiving enough to keep her and their son safe.

LISCNM0618

When Chase McLear is accused of aiding the Red Rose Killer, can Maisy Lockwood, the daughter of one of the victims, help him clear his name before they both become targets?

Read on for a sneak preview of
STANDING FAST by **Maggie K. Black**,
the next book in the **MILITARY K-9 UNIT** *miniseries,*
available July 2018 from Love Inspired Suspense!

The scream was high-pitched and terrified, sending Senior Airman Chase McLear shooting straight out of bed like a bullet from a gun. Furious howls from his K-9 beagle, Queenie, sounded the alarm that danger was near. Chase's long legs propelled him across the floor. He felt the muscles in his arms tense for an unknown battle, as the faces of the brave men and women who'd been viciously killed by Boyd Sullivan, the notorious Red Rose Killer, flickered like a slide show through his mind.

Sudden pain shot through his sole as his bare foot landed hard on one of the wooden building blocks his daughter, Allie, had left scattered across the floor. He grabbed the door frame and blinked hard. His three-year-old daughter was crying out in her sleep from her bedroom down the hall.

Seemed they were both having nightmares tonight.

He started down the hall toward her, ignoring the stinging pain in his foot.

"No!" His daughter's tiny panicked voice filled the darkened air.

"It's okay, Allie! Everything's going to be okay. Daddy's coming!" He reached her room. There in the gentle glow of a night-light was his daughter's tiny form tossing and turning on top of her blankets. Her eyes were still scrunched tightly in sleep.

A loud crack outside yanked his attention to the window at his right. He leaped to his feet and started for the glass just in time to see the blur of a figure rush away through the bushes. His heart pounded like a war drum in his rib cage as he threw open the window. The screen had been slit with what looked like a knife and peeled back, as if someone had tried to get inside

He closed the window firmly, locking it in place. Then he looked down at Queenie. "Stay here. Protect Allie."

Don't miss
STANDING FAST by Maggie K. Black,
available July 2018 wherever
Love Inspired® Suspense books and ebooks are sold.

www.LoveInspired.com

Looking for inspiration in tales
of hope, faith and heartfelt romance?

Check out **Love Inspired**® and
Love Inspired® **Suspense** books!

New books available every month!

CONNECT WITH US AT:

Harlequin.com/Community

Facebook.com/HarlequinBooks

Twitter.com/HarlequinBooks

Instagram.com/HarlequinBooks

Pinterest.com/HarlequinBooks

ReaderService.com

LIGENRE2018